The
In-Between

Also by Rebecca K. S. Ansari

The Missing Piece of Charlie O'Reilly

The
In-Between

Rebecca K. S. Ansari

WALDEN POND PRESS

An Imprint of HarperCollinsPublishers

Walden Pond Press is an imprint of HarperCollins Publishers.

Walden Pond Press and the skipping stone logo are trademarks and registered trademarks of Walden Media, LLC.

The In-Between

Library of Control Control Number: 2020947621

ISBN 978-0-06-291610-5

Typography by Dana Fritts

22 23 24 25   PC/BRR   10 9 8 7 6 5 4 3 2

❖

First paperback edition, 2022

To my parents, Carol and Roger, whose love of books and reading never faltered, even when mine did

1

The girl was staring at him again.

Like she had every day since moving into the house across the alley three months ago, the slight, pale girl sat perched on her new tree swing, swaying gently, her eyes prying into Cooper's life. It was normally annoying, bordering on creepy even, but today, her presence only served to enrage him further as he exploded out of his back door, the sickening news his mother had shared ricocheting around in his skull. Seeing the girl there, Cooper bellowed, "Can't you just leave me alone?"

He already knew she wouldn't answer. She never did. Her expression didn't change one bit. She simply looked up and down the alley, as if checking to make sure they were alone, before settling her eyes on him again.

Cooper kicked a dog-chewed tennis ball that had somehow ended up in his driveway, sending it like a missile against the garage door. It almost hit him on the rebound, and he had to awkwardly dodge it. He flushed furiously, both with embarrassment and at the thought of what the girl was about to witness.

A stiff Chicago October wind tore a wave of yellowed leaves from their branches, raining them down on him as he pulled his father's pocket watch from his jeans. For a fraction of a second, he hesitated. Oh, how Cooper loved this watch. He used to sneak it from his father's bedside table and bring it back to his room, where he would press the gold plunger at the top to open the cover and feel the soft click of the latch as he shut it, over and over, the sensation simple, satisfying, and comforting. Cooper had always imagined its original owner, his great-great-grandfather, doing the same, checking the time on his way to the bank, or the train, or wherever people went back then. "You are the next in a long line of Stewart men to have this," his father had said with pride when he'd finally gifted it to Cooper. Cooper hadn't known yet that being a Stewart man was nothing to be proud of.

How stupid he'd been. It was a dumb watch. Just another thing his father had ruined.

He opened the cover for the last time. The chain coiled on the cement beneath it as he set the watch on the ground with a gentle care that came by habit—rather ironic now. In the back corner of the garage, Cooper grabbed a cobweb-covered baseball bat from its home amid the collection of neglected sporting gear. The bat had been another gift from his father, and Cooper had told his mom months ago that she could throw it away. Now he was glad she hadn't listened to him.

Back when his parents were still married, Cooper hadn't known which was worse: the many times his dad was too busy working to show up to his games with all the other parents, or the times his dad did manage to make it, shouting endless, useless bits of advice from the stands every time Cooper came to the plate. *Choke up on the bat! Step into it! See yourself making contact!*

Finally he could put those words to good use.

Cooper walked back out to the driveway and smiled grimly as he placed his feet the way his dad had shown him. He tapped the tip of the bat to the shiny glass face of the watch, his other hand up in the air, signaling to an imaginary umpire for time as he stepped into position. He glanced quickly across the alley to make sure the girl had a good view as he wrapped both hands around the grip and raised the bat over his head. With a wail, he brought it down.

One hit would have been plenty. But Cooper struck the mangled pieces over and over again, each hit punctuated with a cry. Springs, gears, and shards of glass shot in all directions. He felt a small cut across his ankle from a flying bit of metal, but he didn't stop even when nothing remained at the spot he continued to pound. The clang of aluminum on cement rang across the neighborhood like a church bell.

Only when the jarring in his hands and shoulders screamed for him to stop did he let the bat clatter to the ground. Then quite unexpectedly Cooper crumpled down beside it. In an instant, his proud fury turned to humiliation, as he was powerless to stop the pathetic display of tears that overcame him. And with them came the same question he'd been asking for three years:

Why, Dad?

How could the same person who used to chase him and his sister around the house to blow raspberries on their stomachs shed his whole family, like he was a hermit crab ditching an old shell? How could he slip into a new life just as easily, with a new wife and a new kid, as if Cooper, Jess, and their mom were just some bad dream he had? Was his father chasing that kid around right now, celebrating the fact that there was about to be a new baby brother or sister in the house? Cooper was sure the scene was happier there than it had been in his kitchen a minute ago, when his mother had shared that same news with him and Jess. But at least Mom had told them this time.

Just you wait, Cooper thought grimly to his unborn half-sibling. *Someday he'll ditch you too.* He covered his face to hide a fresh wave of sobs in case the girl across the alley was still watching. He tried to swallow them down, choke them back, gagging from the effort.

Then came the second question he'd been asking himself for almost as long: *Why do I still care?* He'd sworn he would never let his dad hurt him again; his father didn't deserve *any* feelings from Cooper. None.

And yet.

Cooper's tears dried over the next many minutes, and he lifted his head to see watch debris scattered around him. A gust of wind blew another flurry of leaves down the alley, dragging their brittle edges against the cracked asphalt. A black bird flew overhead, cawing loudly. Cooper watched it sail past and wiped at his cheeks before slowly rising and brushing off the back of his pants.

All of that, and he felt no better.

He looked across the alley, to see if his violent outburst had satisfied the girl's seemingly unending interest in him. If it had, it didn't show. She just continued to swing, lightly and calmly, her eyes never unlocking from him as the rope creaked against the bark of the large bough. The prim private-school uniform she always wore—a navy-blue skirt and blazer with gold-stitched crest—remained unruffled.

"What'd you think?" Cooper asked loudly against the wind. "Did you enjoy the show? Don't forget to tip your server."

She said nothing.

The irony of it was not lost on Cooper. He hadn't known anyone could be less interested in making friends than he was.

He looked beyond her, to her house, newly restored, clean, and expensive, the nicest house on the block. He'd never seen the sibling who lived in the second of two upstairs bedrooms with the windows that faced his house; Cooper assumed it was a sister who was much messier than this girl. He'd never seen the girl's parents either, who he assumed left early for work and came home late from their clearly well-paying jobs.

They had transformed the previously abandoned house into a gorgeous home in a flash, it seemed, like on one of those reality TV shows; Cooper, Jess, and their mother had gone on a summer trip to their grandparents, and when they had returned, the makeover was complete. Butter-yellow paint had replaced the previous chipped brown siding, and new windows sparkled where dusty broken panes had previously let in the rain and wind. The yard was flush with thick grass and potted plants instead of the previous dirt and trash, and down the path from the rebuilt wraparound porch was—no joke—an actual white picket fence.

When Cooper's family had arrived home from that trip, he had marveled at how amazing the house looked, but then the look in his mother's eyes made him immediately regret saying anything. Their own house desperately needed new paint and windows, two of the many things his parents had said they were going to renovate when they bought a cheap house in a neighborhood that was supposed to be on the rise. They had managed a new roof and heating system over the years, but then his father had left—moving with his new wife to a pristine suburb that didn't need to rise. It was already at the top.

His mom's only response was a sigh and, "Okay, Cooper . . ."

As for their neighborhood, it never did end up rising. And after that day a few months ago, Cooper never mentioned the house across the alley to his mother again, even though everything about the house seemed perfect.

Everything, that is, except the quiet girl with the cheerless stare.

Slowly, with eyes that burned from the cutting wind, Cooper backed away. That was when the girl nodded once at him, almost imperceptibly, like granting him leave. It sent a chill down his spine. He turned and quickly climbed the cement steps to his back door. As he turned the knob, he took one last glance back.

He blinked to make sure he was seeing clearly, and his breath caught in his throat. Cooper had only looked away for an instant, but now, across the alley, all he saw was a gently swaying empty swing. The girl was gone.

2

"Dinner's ready," Cooper's mother said as he entered the kitchen.

"Can you grab the milk?" Jess asked quietly.

Cooper just blinked at them both. Dinner prep? Milk? That's all they were concerned with after the news Mom had delivered? And there was no way they hadn't heard Cooper's destruction out on the driveway. Yet Jess hadn't moved from her spot at the kitchen table where she'd been working on her math homework, and Mom was busying herself at the stove, silent.

Cooper opened the refrigerator door and stood blinking at the cold white space for almost a full minute, his mind so fuzzy and full that he had already forgotten why he was there.

"The milk?" Jess said again.

"Right," Cooper mumbled. The yellow cap of the plastic jug, screwed on poorly after breakfast that morning, flew through the air as he plopped the half-full gallon onto the table.

"Cooper!" Jess flinched, glaring at him.

"Oh, *that* upsets you?"

"Please, put it down more gently next time," his mother said, taking a seat. "There's no need to slam it."

"Yeah," Jess said.

"I didn't slam it. I just . . ." Cooper slid into his space at the table and shut his mouth as his mom dropped his plate in front of him.

Eggs again.

Cooper had nothing against eggs. In fact, he used to love them. But even an egg fanatic would tire of how often they were served in the Stewart home. Boiled, scrambled, fried; breakfast, lunch, dinner. This was life with a diabetic sister and an overworked vegetarian mother. "Protein is key," the diabetes doctors had told them when Jess was diagnosed four years before. Jess, who had previously lived on mac and cheese and Fruity Pebbles, had to adjust to a slew of new dietary rules.

They'd all learned a lot since then. Jess had learned that her body could no longer turn food into energy without multiple daily shots of a hormone called insulin. In order to see how much insulin she needed, she also had to prick her finger before *every single shot* to test how much sugar was in her blood. On a bad day, it would add up to more than twenty needle pokes.

Cooper had learned that jabbing his then-six-year-old sister led to lots of fights and tears. Diabetes refused to take a day off, no matter how hard Jess begged. The *pop-click* of Mom piercing Jess's fingertip with a lancet—a little needle that shot out from its plastic casing—became as familiar a sound to Cooper as his mother's voice.

Mom, meanwhile, had learned a dozen new ways to make eggs and soothe Jess's tears. And their dad had learned a hundred new ways to vanish. He played with them less, helped them with their homework even less, and started working late, going out with buddies, or staring silently at the TV for hours on end.

"When will you be home tonight?" Jess asked their mother now, through a mouthful of scrambled eggs.

"Same as every Monday, honey."

"So, what time?"

"Ten o'clock," Cooper said. "Her pottery class starts at seven thirty and ends at nine thirty. Just like last week. And

11

the week before that. And the week before that. And the week—"

"But do you *have* to teach tonight?" Jess said, ignoring him. "You're always gone."

"I'm not always gone. It's only three nights a week."

"I don't get why you have to teach at all. You already work all day."

Their mom put her fork down and rubbed her face with both hands. Cooper glared at his sister; the only thing that kept him from yelling, "Stop being so stupid!" was knowing it would only make Mom more upset. Officially, he didn't know that his father was sending the smallest amount of money possible within the rules of the divorce; he didn't know his mother was struggling to pay for their house and groceries, or that she had no choice but to pick up a second job teaching classes at the arts center in addition to her day job as a massage therapist.

He didn't know a lot of things, *officially*, but the wall between Cooper's and his mother's bedroom was much thinner than she realized. After listening to enough of his parents' late-night phone calls, Cooper didn't know which was worse: silence or screaming. Cooper got one from his father; his mother got the other.

His mom laced her fingers under her chin and lifted the corners of her mouth in something that resembled a smile.

"So! Cooper, how was school today?"

"Fine."

"Did you turn in those late assignments?"

"Yup," he lied.

"What else did you do?"

"You know. Classes and stuff."

She let out a loud breath. "And how's Zack?"

"Fine."

"And Remi?"

"Good."

"They haven't been over in a while."

Cooper shrugged. "They're busy."

His mom waited for more, but there was really nothing else to say. They were fine. At least, as far as Cooper could tell from his silent seat at the lunch table. He'd probably know more if he went to the movies or the sleepovers his friends invited him to, though it had been so long since Cooper had accepted that they barely even asked anymore. Only Zack, Cooper's was-best-friend, still tried to talk to him every day, but that was probably only because he lived across the street.

If the sole person you spend time with is yourself, no one can disappoint you.

With a sigh, his mother chose to move on. "And how about you, Jess?"

"We did the coolest thing in science today!"

Cooper closed his eyes in relief as Jess went on and on about her classes, her teachers, her plans for her and her friends' group Halloween costume. At least her blathering meant he didn't have to say a word as she recounted who said what about who, who liked who, who wasn't speaking to who, and who was upset about what. Cooper was consistently amazed that she could spend this much energy caring about such unimportant things. It was shocking her blood sugar didn't drop from the effort.

He finished, cleared his plate, and grabbed his backpack. "I'm going to do some homework, Mom. Can you let me know when you leave?"

His mother looked at the oven clock and said, "Oh no, I should have left already! Can you clear my dishes?"

He put his bag back down. "Sure."

As she hurried over to where her jacket hung, she nearly tripped over a large mesh cylinder sitting in the corner of the room. "Jess, can I get rid of that yet?"

"No! She's going to hatch. She just needs more time."

"Your cocoon's dead," Cooper said.

"It is *not*," Jess snapped. "And it's a *chrysalis*, not a cocoon!"

The booklet that had come with Jess's Giant Butterfly

14

Garden had promised three to five monarchs in two weeks, but only one of Jess's caterpillars had even managed to make a chrysalis, and that one had been dangling there for almost two months.

"Fine. Your *chrysalis* is dead. You should email them and get your money back."

"She is *not* dead!"

"Totally dead."

"Mom!"

Cooper's mother gave him a look while she pulled her jacket on before turning to Jess with a gentle tilt of the head. "Honey, your brother might be right. Maybe it got too cold or something."

"She just needs more time," Jess repeated with her nose in the air and a firm nod.

Cooper rolled his eyes. His mom kissed Jess's cheek, then almost hit Cooper in the face with her messenger bag as she threw the cross-body strap over her head.

"Will you come kiss me when you get home?" Jess said.

"Of course I will, sweetie," Mom said. "Cooper, can you text me her blood sugar at bedtime?"

"Yeah." *Like always.* When exactly, he wondered, would Jess be able to check her own blood sugar? He had started helping with her diabetes when *he* was ten, so why couldn't

15

Jess do it now that she was? Oh, right, if Jess learned to manage her diabetes herself, she'd lose all the attention. Cooper was quite certain she didn't want that.

He looked up at his mother, and knew, at that moment, if he leaned forward even so much as a millimeter, his mom would envelop him in a hug. And yet, despite feeling a tug in his chest as surely as a rope tied to his heart, he leaned away instead.

His mom's lips pinched together, and she nodded. "Love you, bud."

He nodded in return.

Cooper rinsed his mother's plate in the sink and watched her roll her bike from the garage, its blinking red taillight flashing as she kicked her leg up and over the saddle. She then expertly dodged the innumerable potholes in their alley on her way to the street and vanished around the turn. Cooper let his eyes drift to the yard across the alley.

"Geez!" He startled, adrenaline flooding his senses. Yes, it was dark out, but Cooper could have sworn the swing had been empty when his mom pulled away. But now there she was. The girl. Sitting. Swinging. Staring right at him.

Cooper reached up and pulled the cord to drop the shade over the window. He was not only a little spooked by her; he was also embarrassed. He didn't mind everyone knowing how angry he was these days—he actually wore it with pride—but no one should know about the crying. The pain. The girl had seen too much.

Block her out, he told himself. *Block everyone out.*

3

Cooper turned quickly to go to his room. Then came a searing pain in his leg and Jess's surprised scream.

It was the freezer door. Jess had opened it behind him, and he hadn't noticed; now his shin was throbbing and Jess, who had been temporarily pinched in the freezer like it was a Venus flytrap, fell from her squatting position onto her rear.

"What are you doing?" Cooper said, rubbing his leg.

Jess glared up at her brother. "You did that on purpose!"

"What are you talking about?" Cooper said. "And what are you doing in the freezer, anyway?"

"Nothing."

"Jess. What's in your hand?"

"Nothing." She showed one free hand before slowly pulling her other from behind her back. There was nothing in it, but a moment later a pint of ice cream rolled into view.

"You can't eat that! Mom already gave you your insulin." It was like Jess *wanted* him to have to text Mom that she had a blood sugar of twelve million.

"I was just going to have *one bite*."

Cooper limped a step, picked up the pint, and tossed it back in the freezer, then waved for Jess to scoot out of the way so he could shut the door. "Look. I'm supposed to make sure you're okay when Mom's gone. The least you could do is not actively make my job harder."

"Oh, I'm sorry. I forgot it was all about you."

"All about *me*?" Cooper said with a laugh. "You're kidding, right?" *Nothing* had been about him since Jess snagged the starring role of "sick kid." Every choice Mom made was about Jess, about what *she* needed. Cooper, meanwhile, was the only person in the family who could smell the syrupy-sweet scent that came on Jess's breath when her sugar became dangerously high. Mom joked that Cooper was as good as one of those expensive medical-service dogs that sniff out trouble before it happens.

As good as a dog.

He walked past his sister without helping her up.

Normally he would head to his room to write about all of today's events in his journal, which always seemed to help him drain his frustrations. But he was too angry. Too hot. Instead, he needed to check out, turn off, disappear.

He headed for his mother's desk, in the corner of the kitchen, but didn't find what he was looking for. He reluctantly turned back to his sister. "Where's Mom's laptop?"

Jess, now standing, straightened the bottom of her shirt and crossed her arms. "Don't you have homework to do?"

"Where's. Mom's. Laptop?" he repeated.

"I don't know. . . . It might be in my room." As Cooper turned to head upstairs, she yelled from behind him, "Mom's going to kill you if you get another D!"

Cooper opened the door to Jess's room. As always, it was pristine. The bed was crisply made (*What's the point?*) with a mountain of carefully placed stuffed animals on top (*How does she even sleep in all that?*), and not as much as one stray sock could be seen on the floor (*Show-off!*). Mr. Miggins, Jess's four-foot-tall teddy bear, sat propped up in the corner. The ridiculously oversized creature had arrived right after Jess was first diagnosed, sitting on her bed when she'd come home from the hospital. Cooper had no idea how that was supposed to help—he always thought Mr. Miggins should have arrived with a note around his neck like Paddington, saying, "I'm so bear-y sorry! You have an incurable illness I can do nothing about!" But Jess loved the thing.

He grabbed the Mac laptop from where it was sitting on Jess's bedside table and crossed the small hallway to his own room, plopping down cross-legged on his bed. He opened the computer and started to close the windows Jess had left open. But before he clicked one red circle, he froze.

It was the Messages app, open to a conversation, though "conversation" was a generous way to put it—only the blue message bubbles on the right were filled in. The most recent read:

Hi, Dad! It's Jess. School started here last month. Fifth grade is supposed to be harder than fourth, but so far, it's been okay. How are you?

Before that:

Hi, Dad! It's Jess. Summer's almost over, but it's still so hot. How's San Diego?

Cooper scrolled up. And up. He saw message after message. Not once had their dad responded. It was as if Jess was texting the wrong person, but Cooper knew the number was right. Dad, apparently, just couldn't be bothered.

"Oh, Jess," he muttered. How many messages had his sister sent into the void? How long would she continue to hope on the hopeless?

He checked his doorway. If she'd walked in, he'd probably have yelled at her or mocked her for being so dumb.

21

But here, alone, he only had sympathy for her. Heartbreak, even.

Cooper too had tried to have contact with his dad when he'd first moved away, writing actual paper letters—short, awkward scrawled notes on stationery his mother had bought him—filled with the same sort of nonsense as Jess's messages. It was the sort of junk you wrote when all you really wanted to ask was *"Why?"* a hundred times over. His dad hadn't responded a single time. Thankfully, Cooper's mother had never asked about the rest of the stationery, because it had long since been reduced to a pile of ash in the backyard.

He strangled the urge to type some rather pointed words to his father right now. The window was open. Instead, Cooper quit the Messages app and whispered once more, "Block him out, Jess."

Cooper intended to watch YouTube, but when he pulled up the internet browser, it was already open to a page with an old black-and-white newspaper article. In the middle was a photo of twisted metal and rubble so deformed that Cooper couldn't even guess at its original shape. Intrigued, he scrolled up to find out what it was, but had to watch the twirling rainbow beach ball for a full minute instead, as the computer, which was almost as old as Jess, refreshed. The article was from a British newspaper called *The Daily News* and was dated October 14, 1928. The words of the banner headline read:

RAILWAY DISASTER IN CHARFIELD! SIXTEEN DEAD

"Wanna play Spit?"

Jess was standing at the door, holding a deck of cards, clearly already over what had happened downstairs. She hated being alone as much as Cooper hated having company.

"Nope."

"Well, what *are* you going to do, then?"

"Why were you reading about a railway disaster?"

He knew his question was an invitation, but he wanted to know. Sure enough, Jess hurried over to his bed and leaped up, landing on her knees. "Can you believe that was a train?" She reached over and scrolled back down to the photos. "That bent metal there, that used to be tracks, and those two curved things were parts of the train wheels. I'm glad all the smoke in the picture makes it hard to see the dead bodies."

"Dead bod— Why is Ms. Chelsea having you read this?" Jess's new teacher did things a little differently—including having her students call her by her first name, which Cooper found weird—but researching such a gruesome accident seemed a little bit much for fifth grade.

"It's just Chelsea, no Ms. And she isn't."

"Then why were you reading this?"

"Because it's a great mystery!" Jess said in a British accent.

"Okay . . ."

"I'm serious. Read it!"

"If I do, will you leave?"

"Yes!" She smiled at him.

He scrolled back to the top. He had to admit, if only to himself, that her excitement was a little contagious.

Early yesterday morning, an overnight train headed for Bristol and bearing fifty people passed a red warning light unheeded. It appears the young engineer never saw the caution light through the thick fog, as all accounts indicate the train never slowed; attempts to brake and avoid the freight train on the tracks at Charfield station ahead of him came too late. In an instant, the train became a tangled knot of steel, splintered wood, and flames.

Locals heard the cacophony of the crash up to six miles away and saw the ensuing inferno climb forty feet into the air. At current count, twenty-three people are injured and sixteen have died. The families of fifteen of the victims have claimed their lost, but one soul remains unidentified.

Firemen found the body of a well-dressed boy, thought
to be twelve or thirteen years old, curled under a seat
in the blackened shell of a third-class cabin. The only
clue to his identity is an insignia on his clothing, but an
immediate search turned up no clue to its origin. Police
are asking for the public's help in identifying this child.

"Well, there you go," Cooper said. "I read it. Bye."

"But you haven't read everything!" She reached across
him again and clicked on a series of other open tabs.

Lost Little Child
The Unsolved Mystery of the 1928 Crash
The Haunting Puzzle of Charfield

"Huh." Cooper tried to sound bored.

"One more?" Jess asked with a grin.

He didn't say yes, but he didn't say no either, so she
linked to another article, one that had been posted only a
year ago, and read from the middle of the text. "No parent
or guardian ever emerged to claim their son, and despite
high-profile efforts made in the decades since, the child
has never been identified. Ninety-two years later, his name
remains a mystery, lost to time." Beside the text was a color
photograph of a tall stone monument in the shape of a cross,

set before a short ivy-covered wall. Jess reached over and pointed to the wide, square pedestal and its weathered and worn words.

In Memory of Those Who Lost Their Lives

A list of names lay beneath these words, only snippets of which were legible.

"Look at the bottom," Jess said.

One Unknown

How is that possible? Cooper wondered. Someone had to have bought the boy's ticket, put him on the train. The original article said he'd been well-dressed, so someone took care of him. Even if he'd been a runaway or a stowaway, someone should have eventually arrived to explain who he was. How could all this time pass without an answer?

"So." Jess grinned at him. "Want to help me solve it?"

"*Solve* it?"

"Yeah!"

Cooper closed the laptop. "Did you not read the articles, Jess? People have been trying to figure this out for almost a century. What makes you think you could do any better?"

"The insignia."

"What insignia?"

Jess sighed dramatically. "Did you not just read the articles? The one on his clothes, that the people in 1928 couldn't identify!"

"What about it?"

"I've seen it before."

Cooper laughed. "Sure you have."

"I have! And so have you. Don't you recognize it?"

Cooper shook his head slowly. "I don't even know what it looks like."

Jess sighed again. "Go back! It's in the first article."

Cooper slowly opened the laptop and navigated back. Next to the photos of the wreck was a rough pencil sketch made by some long-dead newspaper artist. It appeared incomplete, only the top half of an image. The caption below read, "Any persons with knowledge of this crest should contact police immediately."

"They couldn't draw the bottom half because it was burned in the fire," Jess said. "But you recognize the top, right?"

There was something familiar about it—the head of a rising bird with two sword tips crossing behind it. But he couldn't place it. He looked at Jess and shrugged, but immediately regretted it when she let out a giggle for knowing something he didn't.

"That girl!" Jess said. "Across the alley. Her jacket has this same symbol."

Her answer made Cooper sit back and pause. He tried to recall the details of the girl's crest, checking his memory against Jess's claim. He had to admit they might be a little similar—at least *half* similar—but he also didn't see what it amounted to. "So?"

"*So*, all we have to do is ask the girl where she got the jacket, find the connection to that kid from 1928, and we'll have solved a nearly hundred-year-old mystery!"

"I doubt it's that simple, Jess."

His sister's eyes were wide with excitement. "We'll be famous. Everyone will want to interview us, ask us how we figured it out. They'll probably fly us to England to accept an award or something. Don't you remember how Dad always wanted to take us to England?"

Ah. So that was what this was all about. Cooper closed the laptop again and laced his fingers together.

"For one," he said, "I doubt the symbols are actually the same. And two, even if they are, and you, *miraculously*, are the first person to finally solve the mystery of the dead kid, it isn't going to make Dad coming running back to us."

Jess sat back heavily on her heels and glared at her brother. "That's not what I was saying."

"It's what you were *thinking*, though."

"You don't know what I'm thinking," she said, but the way she blinked and turned away said otherwise.

"It won't matter, Jess. He doesn't care."

The lower lids of his sister's eyes reddened as she looked back at him and spoke very slowly. "What is wrong with you?"

"I'm just telling the truth."

"You're so mean! You are terrible and cold and. . . mean!"

"You already said mean."

Jess pushed off his bed and started to walk away.

"The sooner you stop caring about him," Cooper said after her, "the sooner it'll stop hurting."

She spun, eyes like slits. "So I can be like you? You don't care about anyone! You're like a robot."

"Yeah, well, at least you don't hear me whining about my feelings."

"That's because you *have* no feelings!"

"Maybe when Dad shows up to take you to England, he can explain it to you."

"Dad, Dad, Dad! You blame everything on him."

"Yeah, well, he ruined our lives, so . . ."

"At least Dad only hurt me once. You do it every day."

"Only once, huh?" Cooper laughed. "What about all those unanswered text messages?"

Jess froze, eyes glistening. Cooper couldn't tell if she was more upset that he'd looked at her messages or that he was cruelly shoving them in her face. Then she howled in out-rage.

"You're *just* like him! You can't deal, so you've *quit* on me and Mom."

Cooper flung the laptop onto his bed and shot up. "No! Don't you *ever* compare me to him!" He felt his fingernails digging painfully into his palms. "GET OUT!"

Slowly, the corners of Jess's mouth turned up, and she crossed her arms. "The sooner you stop caring, the sooner it'll stop hurting," she mocked before turning and walking out.

Cooper slammed the door behind her and paced a few times before throwing a book against the wall. It didn't matter how mean he was. He could be mean to his sister all day every day, and it would never come close to what his father had done.

Cooper and his dad were *not* the same. He took a deep breath and tried to wipe his mind clear.

Forget what Jess said.

Forget about his dad's new baby.

Pack it all away.

Do something else.

He sat down, opened the computer again, and turned reality off.

4

"Yo!" Zack said as Cooper plopped onto the vinyl bus seat beside him.

"Hey," Cooper said. He sank slowly as air sighed out of the seams of the cushion, bringing with it a musty, old-foam odor.

"Man," Zack said, "I stayed up *waaaay* too late last night. Tyler and I finally found a good group and finished that raid in Destiny."

Cooper didn't even know what raid his friend was talking about—it had been months since he'd last logged on to the video game Zack and his older brother were apparently still playing. When Zack held his hand up for a congratulatory high five, though, Cooper weakly complied.

They had been best friends since before Cooper could remember, and even if they hadn't really hung out in a long time, they still knew things about each other that no one else did. Cooper kept Zack's secret that he still hid a Beanie Baby kitten in his pillowcase. Zack was the one who, one morning at sleepaway camp, had only needed one glance at Cooper's terrified face to "playfully" dump his entire water bottle on Cooper and his sheets. Cooper still had no clue how Zack knew he'd wet the bed, but Zack's quick thinking had saved him from everyone seeing that his cot was soaked. They'd never talked about it. They didn't have to. They had each other's backs.

Or at least they used to.

Cooper and Zack had also never talked about the chasm that now lay between them. It had grown so gradually. Zack knew Cooper's dad wasn't around anymore, of course. Cooper had told Zack that he didn't want to talk about it, but when it was all Cooper could think about, that meant not talking to Zack about anything at all. Now it seemed too late. Cooper was sure that, even if he tried, Zack could never truly understand him anymore. Zack's life was too . . . easy. He didn't have to deal with any of the garbage Cooper did. His parents were the sort of people who kissed in public and still giggled at each other's lame jokes.

Giggled.

No. There was no way Zack could get it.

Now Zack gently elbowed him in the ribs. "I know why I look rough, but what's your excuse?"

"Oh, Jess and I got into a fight." Cooper said this dismissively, but he had tossed and turned in bed past midnight hearing the echoes of all he'd said, feeling like a jerk (though he knew he'd probably say it all over again if Jess came back at him). When he'd gone to her room to check her blood sugar before bedtime, she wouldn't even speak to him. This silence wasn't broken at breakfast, and when they left for the bus, she had run ahead to meet up with her friends. "It's no biggy, though," he added.

"What'd you fight about?"

"Nothing."

A quiet descended between the two of them, making Cooper wiggle in his seat and chew his fingernail. Two years ago, Cooper would have been excited to tell Zack about that train mystery, the unidentified boy and crest and the possible connection to the girl next door. In fact, he probably would have texted Zack the night before, the minute after Jess showed him the articles. But nothing seemed to want to come out of his mouth anymore. Words and thoughts seemed to get lodged in the back of his throat, tangled and stuck like a logjam.

So Cooper just sat, half paying attention as Zack filled the empty air with what had happened in the video game. He listened, nodding at the appropriate times, and even managed a few "Cool" and "Wow" comments along the way, but his mind wandered. Was it possible that the girl across the alley was connected to that crash somehow? It didn't make any sense how she could be, but the crests *were* awfully similar. . . .

With a squeal and a lurch, the bus came to its next stop. Two seventh-grade girls boarded, discussing something of great seriousness as they took their seats a few rows ahead of Cooper. They were followed by two younger brothers and a new boy in Cooper's grade who wore the exact same thing every day: a pair of khakis and a baggy sweatshirt that read CALM DOWN! IT'S PE, NOT THE OLYMPICS. Cooper's mom would describe this kid as "big-boned," which Cooper always found to be a weird phrase, since he was pretty sure everyone's bones were the same size.

As this thought was running through Cooper's head, the boy looked directly at him, causing Cooper to quickly turn away, feeling like a jerk for musing about his bones one way or another. By the time Cooper glanced back, the boy had sat down in no-man's-land.

By official school policy, the first two rows were for

the kindergartners, and the rest of the bus was open for all. Everyone knew, however, the unspoken bus rules: the older you were, and the cooler you were, the farther you got to sit to the back. Everyone sorted themselves out accordingly, but since there were more seats on the bus than there were kids, there were always at least two or three empty rows between the kindergartners and everyone else.

The new kid always sat in row three.

"Those two are like identical twins attached at the head!" one of Cooper's classmates joked loudly, nodding toward the chatting girls. "Hey, ladies! Do you need to be surgically detached, or do you share only one brain?"

There were snickers from the whole back row. One of the girls stared pointedly forward, ignoring the barb. The other gave the entire back of the bus a squinty-eyed glare before swinging her head around with a dramatic whip of her ponytail.

Cooper looked at his new classmate. It was best he was in the front. Up there, he was out of the splash zone of all the eighth-grade jeers and jokes—any closer and he would almost certainly become a target.

As Cooper sat there, jostled by a bad patch of road, he couldn't keep from glancing at the boy, who stared silently out the window at the houses as they rolled by. Cooper had never spoken to this kid, but they didn't need to talk for Cooper to know they had one thing in common. As he too turned to look out his window to take in the view, the familiar weight of loneliness pressed down on both of them.

5

An unusually long line stretched out the door of the lunchroom and down the hallway when Cooper arrived after math, lunch bag in hand. He had tried to sneak into the library to use the computers while he ate, but the librarian was like a hawk when it came to food—she could smell even an apple from a mile away. Further research on the train mystery would have to wait. .

"Cooper!" Zack flagged him over from his place halfway down the line. "Over here."

"What's going on?" Cooper stood on tiptoes and peered toward the kitchen to see what was causing the holdup.

"Alicia said something went wrong with the plumbing

this morning, so they're way behind getting lunch ready. Wanna jump in line with us?" He grinned. "You'll basically get a free late pass to science."

"Nah." Cooper shook his head. "I'm good." He held up his lunch bag and turned away. Not only did he have the sandwich he'd packed, but he'd also stopped at the vending machine to supplement his meal with a few non-diabetic-approved snacks.

The smell of sanitizer and the ever-lingering odor of a thousand lunches past greeted Cooper as he made his way between the cafeteria tables. They were sparsely populated at the moment, basically just the other brown baggers. He sat at their usual table and pulled out his lunch, his journal, and his favorite pencil, now just a stub, one sharpening away from death.

Only one sentence in, however, there came a voice from across the table.

"Is it okay if I sit here?"

The kid from the bus stood before him. Cooper hastily covered what he was writing before glancing side to side at the open chairs.

"It's okay if you're saving seats for someone else," the boy said, and started to turn away.

"No. I mean, no, I'm not saving seats."

The boy smiled slightly. "May I?"

"Sure."

The boy pulled out a chair. "I'm Gus."

Cooper closed his journal and moved his lunch bag to the side. "I'm Cooper." He'd never had a good look at the boy's face before, mostly just the back of his head on the bus. Gus had acne that looked painful, and also braces, which Cooper guessed were new because his lips didn't seem used to them yet.

"So, how's it going?" Gus asked a bit awkwardly.

"Good . . . pretty good," Cooper said reflexively. When the ensuing silence became uncomfortable, Cooper added, "You're new this year, right?"

"Yeah."

"How's that going?"

"It's been . . . somethin'," Gus said with a shrug and a small grimace.

Cooper nodded, because he knew what Gus really meant: *It's awful and I don't really want to talk about it.* He changed the subject. "Where'd you go to school last year?"

"Westminster." When Cooper gave him a quick head shake, Gus added, "Oh, sorry. It's in Oklahoma City. That's where I really live. I came to Chicago to stay with my grandma for a bit until my parents can get some things worked out."

Cooper knew all about parents getting "things worked

39

out." He hoped Gus's parents were better at it than his own had been.

That's when he remembered where Gus got on the bus. "Wait," he asked cautiously. "Who's your grandma?"

"Virginia Dreffel," Gus answered.

Cooper groaned. He couldn't help it. The neighborhood kids called her Ms. Dreadful. The first time he'd walked by her house, he had mistakenly touched a blade of her grass and she'd waved her cane in the air and shouted, "Get off my lawn!" Cooper had assumed she was joking. Did anyone *actually* say that?

Apparently Ms. Dreadful did. She had a NO TRES-PASSING sign hanging on the handrail leading to her front door, and each Halloween, she strung a line of yellow tape across the end of her driveway with the word CAU-TION repeated in big black lettering—not in a decorative haunted-house kind of way, but more in an I'll-call-the-cops kind of way. It was like she didn't know that if you didn't want trick-or-treaters, all you had to do was turn off your lights and ignore the doorbell.

Cooper immediately felt bad for groaning, but Gus just laughed. Cooper's reaction clearly wasn't much of a surprise.

"I didn't know Ms. Dreffel even had kids," said Cooper, "let alone grandkids."

"Yeah, my grandpa died right after my mom was born.

My mom's tried to convince me that my grandma has a good heart, but *she* moved out the minute she turned eighteen, so . . ." He made a face even more dour than Cooper's had been. "They don't talk all that much."

"But they still sent you to live there?" Cooper said.

"No other choice, apparently. You could come over sometime, if you want."

Cooper froze at the thought. He didn't know how to answer; he just opened and closed his mouth a few times. Gus started laughing again, this time loud and warm. "I'm kidding! Oh, man. I wish you could see your face. You're all like," and he made a face like someone in a Halloween scare house.

At that, Cooper couldn't help laughing as well, Gus's face was so funny and his laughter so infectious. Gus made a few more frightened faces, each more ridiculous than the last, cracking them both up. Cooper felt a lightness in his chest that was foreign and familiar at the same time. It had been a long time since he'd laughed like this.

Eventually their laughter died down, and Gus started to eat again. He nodded at Cooper's journal. "What're you writing? Is that for school?"

Cooper flicked a glance down at his notebook before pulling it onto his lap. "Um, no. It's just . . . stuff." He found an intense new interest in his lunch, rearranging the PB&J,

granola bar, and Snickers before taking a big bite of sand-wich.

Gus seemed to take the hint. "Man, I wish my grandma packed me lunches like that!"

When it came to picking his meal selections, Cooper regularly took a wrecking ball to the food pyramid. "Yeah, I guess there are some benefits to packing my own lunch."

"I want to live with your parents."

Cooper snorted. "Nah. You just need to know where the vending machines are. And it's 'parent.' Singular."

"Oh."

"Yeah," Cooper said with a quick shake of his head. "It's tough with my dad overseas, but someone has to fight for our country, right?" The lie fell out of his mouth before he could stop it.

"Your dad's in the army?"

"Marines."

"Wow! Where is he?"

Cooper looked past Gus to the back wall of the lunch-room and said, "Afghanistan."

"Oh, man. How often do you get to see him?"

"I don't." At least that part was true. "He and my mom are divorced, and I don't really get to talk to him that much."

Cooper knew he should stop right there, say something like "Nah, just kidding," before telling Gus that his dad was a cardiologist who hadn't spent a second in the military. But the whole reason he'd lied in the first place was because marines have a good reason to not be around. Cooper imagined marines were too busy saving the world to send birthday cards or gifts. Marines could entirely disappear from your life admirably, right?

"My dad's not around much either," Gus said. "Both of my parents travel a ton; only one of them's ever really home at a time. They've always told me that being away makes them love me even more, but since it seems to have made them love each other less. . . ."

Cooper stayed quiet. His lie seemed to have hardened into something he couldn't take back; meanwhile, Gus had told him something honest and personal. His stomach suddenly felt as wriggly as a bag of worms.

"Do you wanna trade?" Gus asked with a wry grin, offering a bag of tired-looking baby carrots while eyeing Cooper's Snickers bar.

Cooper wasn't even hungry anymore. "No, thanks. But you can have it, if you want."

Gus's face lit up, like it was the nicest thing anyone had ever said to him. "Really?"

"Sure." Cooper tossed the Snickers bar across the table.

"I'm the same, by the way," Gus said, opening the wrapper.

"The kid of a marine?" Cooper's throat tightened. What would he say if Gus asked any questions that required actual knowledge of the military?

"No, a journaler. I mean I like to write too."

Cooper exhaled. "Oh! For real? You mean, like, stories?"

"Sometimes. But usually, you know, random things. Ideas. Drawings. You?"

"Yeah, the same, I—"

"Cooper!" Zack's voice sailed across the cafeteria. "We're coming, man!" Cooper turned around to see him waving his arms in the air; he'd finally gotten to the front of the check-out line. "We got our food! Just in time for graduation!" Zack, Remi, and a bunch of the soccer team laughed from behind him.

Cooper turned back around and took a quick count of the number of seats left at the table. With Gus taking a spot, there wasn't enough room for everyone he normally sat with.

Gus must have sensed what was happening, because the easy smile on his face dimmed. The warmth that had buoyed the hot-air balloon of their conversation was gone. "It's okay," he said before Cooper even opened his mouth. He packed the remains of his lunch into a crumpled brown bag that had been used so many times it looked as soft as fabric and pushed his chair away from the table with a screech. "I'm done anyway."

"You don't, I mean—" Cooper began.

"I'll see you later." Gus walked away.

"Yeah. Later."

Cooper sagged in his seat. How had he screwed that up so badly? He could have pulled up another chair, or made room, or at least not acted like sitting with Gus was only an option if no one else was available.

Zack and the rest of the crew descended on the table, midconversation, laughing, bringing with them the smell of meat loaf, gravy, and cooked carrots. "Finally!" Zack said. "Sorry to leave you alone like that."

Cooper watched Gus in case he turned around before disappearing out the cafeteria door, but he didn't. It had actually been the least alone Cooper had felt in a long time.

6

The cafeteria was back to normal the next day, so any lingering hope Cooper had of some easy time with Gus again was dashed. Cooper saw him in the hallways a few times and caught his eye with a smile and a small wave, but Gus simply nodded and kept walking.

On the bus home, Cooper watched the back of Gus's head, bobbing up and down with each bump in the road, alone up there in no-man's-land. When they reached the bus stop in front of Ms. Dreffel's darkened house, Gus was the last one to walk down the stairs. He stalled on the sidewalk, looking up at his grandmother's home, seeming to gird himself before weaving through unkept bushes and climbing the front steps.

A few minutes later, Jess, Cooper, and Zack got off at their own stop. Jess hadn't said more than a few words to Cooper since Monday evening, and she crossed the street to their home without so much as a glance Cooper's way.

"You want to come over?" Zack asked. "We could play Xbox or watch a movie or something?"

"Nah," Cooper said as the school bus pulled away. "I've got a ton of homework."

"You sure? My dad could make us his famous popcorn."

Not going to happen. "Maybe tomorrow," Cooper offered.

"Sure," Zack said.

Cooper, Jess, and Mom went through their normal Wednesday evening routine: homework, eggs, a promise to text Jess's blood sugar to their mom, and then Mom biking off to her pottery class. Cooper found the whole thing both boring and comforting.

He settled into his room with his mother's laptop again, with every intention of watching a video, but he found his fingers frozen in midair above the keyboard. The sketch of the crest with the bird and swords was still knocking at a little door in his mind. Was it really the same insignia on the girl's jacket next door? Every school crest kind of looked the same. And even if they were identical, it didn't mean he or Jess could figure out who that kid in the train crash was ninety years ago.

Right?

An idea crossed his mind. He batted it away, given it was accompanied by a queasy feeling in his stomach, but it refused to be ignored.

Just one good look across the alley. He wasn't a creep or a stalker or whatever if he was simply seeking information. It was only to get a clear look at that crest, for comparison's sake, that's all. Just to rule it out, so he wouldn't have to think about it anymore. Besides, she stared at him all the time, right? It wasn't that different.

Cooper scrambled off the bed and dragged a water-stained end table that used to hold his fish tank over to the windowsill. Then he pulled a huge telescope from the top shelf of his closet, its weight threatening to crush him. Grandma Stewart had dropped nearly a thousand dollars a few years ago on the thing, with hopes Cooper would be the next Carl Sagan after he watched one old episode of *Cosmos*. But the only thing the telescope had discovered so far was the *billions and billions* of dust bunnies that lived in his closet.

Grandma Stewart would never know that, of course, because she didn't come around any more often than his dad did. She'd only come to the house once anyway, and wouldn't stop talking about a man she had passed at the corner who was asking for spare change. From then on, Cooper and Jess only saw her when they visited her at her gated community, where she often wondered aloud at how *interesting* it was that her son had married someone *from such a different background* as their mother.

What Grandma Stewart was really saying was *poor*.

Cooper grunted as he set the telescope down on the end table and aimed it toward the girl's house. As he peered into the eyepiece and fiddled with a truly excessive number of knobs, a blurry smear of yellow morphed into crisp focus, and the texture of the siding on the house across the alley became clearly detailed. Cooper looked out the window with his naked eye and angled the viewer toward the girl's upstairs bedroom.

After more small adjustments to the scope, Cooper finally found himself focused within the room, which was lit but thankfully unoccupied. Slowly he scanned side to side, amazed at the level of detail he could see. What from afar he'd thought were polka dots on her puffy comforter and matching pillow mountain were actually small stitched rosebuds. He could read the spines of the packed bookshelf—*A Wrinkle in Time, When You Reach Me, Harry Potter and the Prisoner of Azkaban*—and he was able to count the six Ticonderoga pencils resting in a mason jar on her desk.

And there, hanging on the back of the desk chair, was the girl's navy-blue jacket.

He adjusted the scope ever so slightly and focused in on the gold stitching. While the folds in the jacket obscured one of the crest's edges, Cooper could make out the embroidery of a large bird, flying upward, wings outstretched, with two swords crossing behind it.

Jess was right. It was exactly like the sketch in the newspaper.

The newspaper sketch had been black and white, but now he could see there was ruby-red stitching in the hilt of each sword that matched a red gleam in the bird's eyes. A banner of some sort was stitched beneath, clutched in the bird's talons. *Vigilantes U—.* The curves in the cloth obscured the letters after.

"Vigilantes?" he whispered to himself. He wasn't sure what that word meant exactly, but he was pretty sure it involved people who took the law into their own hands.

Cooper scanned the room again. He knew he was now pushing the limits of "research." He had already confirmed the crest was a match. He should put the telescope away. But he couldn't stop himself from poking around a little bit more to see if there were any other interesting items in her room. As he did, he passed his view over her desk again.

"Wait. Wha—?"

He zoomed in on the mason jar.

No pencils.

Had someone, somehow, walked into the room while he was checking out the jacket and taken them? He quickly zoomed out again. The room was empty.

Surely he would have seen someone cross the room. How had the pencils simply vanished? There had been six of them just seconds ago. He had counted them! He'd even read the brand. Cooper panned up to the shelf to check the spines of the books again.

"What are you doing?"

Cooper jolted up and away from the scope so fast he almost toppled over backward. He spun around to find Jess, mouth agape in the doorway of his room, the threads of an unfinished friendship bracelet hanging limply in her fingers.

"Nothing!" he shouted, too loudly. He couldn't have appeared any guiltier if he'd tried.

"I can't believe you! You're totally looking at that girl's jacket, aren't you?"

"No." He stuffed his hands in his pockets and looked around his room. The telescope just sat there, pointed at the girl's bedroom window, impossible to explain away.

"Yes, you are! You made fun of *me* and then decided to try to solve the mystery without me?"

"I'm not trying to solve anything. There's nothing to solve. I just wanted to see if they were actually the same, that's all."

"You want to take all the glory for yourself!" She threw the friendship bracelet at him; it fell to the floor limply, halfway between them.

"Jess. There is no *glory*."

"Fine," Jess said. "You *weren't* working on this behind my back. I believe you. You were just peeping into that girl's window for fun, then?" She crossed her arms and smirked.

"You know that's not what I was doing," Cooper said in a hushed voice, even though there wasn't anyone else in the house to hear them.

Jess pantomimed a crass, openmouthed kiss, her hands caressing an invisible body before her.

"Stop that."

"I bet Mom will love hearing about this. I can't wait to tell her." She turned to leave, practically skipping with joy.

"Fine!" he called after her. "I was looking for more information."

Jess stopped and slowly turned back toward him. "And?"

Cooper stifled a frustrated growl. The fact that his little sister held the upper hand stung like an army of fire ants, and it practically killed him to admit that her little mystery had interested him. But it was still better than having his mother think he was some window-leering creep.

"If we work on this together, will you keep your mouth shut to Mom?"

She lifted one eyebrow and tilted her head. "Okay."

"Okay. Here's what I saw." Cooper took some paper from his desk and drew a quick sketch of the emblem as best he could, adding in some of the lower-half details missing from the newspaper image. "The top is identical, but there's a banner at the bottom," he told Jess, "with the word 'Vigilantes' on it, then the letter U, but I couldn't see the rest of the words."

"Vigilantes? What does that mean?"

"A vigilante is someone who . . . hold on." He went to the computer and opened the Merriam-Webster website. "'A member of a volunteer committee organized to suppress or punish crime; a self-appointed doer of justice.' Synonyms include 'punisher' and 'avenger.'"

"Jeez!" Jess said. "What kind of school does she go to?"

"I'm sure the other words we're missing change its meaning." If the girl's insignia was actually the same as the one from the train crash, he and Jess might already have more information to go on than the cops had back in 1928, given that they had almost the entire crest. Cooper handed the computer to his sister. "Let's see if we can find another online match to the crest itself, now that we have more than just the top half. I'm going to go get the iPad so we can both search."

As he went downstairs to fetch the tragically abused and cracked iPad from the living room, a question rose in his mind. Jess was nose down in the computer as he walked in again.

"Hey. How did you just happen to find that article about the train crash in the first place?" he asked. "It's quite a coincidence that you read some random unsolved mystery only to find it might involve our neighbor."

Jess didn't answer.

"Jess?" Cooper said when she stayed quiet. "If we are going to work together, you have to tell me."

"Well . . ." Her voice was small as she said, "I was actually trying to find out more about her."

"The girl across the alley? Why?"

"I just . . . she's . . ." Jess stalled.

"Yes?"

"Well, I was curious. She never talks to us, but she sits there, in that beautiful house, like some glamorous movie star, going off to some fancy private school each day."

Cooper let out a slow sigh. Though it had been a while, this wasn't the first time Jess had expressed a fascination with private school. It began when she was first diagnosed with diabetes, as she begged her parents to let her transfer after a few embarrassing low-blood-sugar incidents. She thought her life would be so much better if she could only get a fresh start, go someplace where no one felt sorry for her or treated her like this poor, fragile thing that might shatter. She failed to see the flaw in her reasoning—diabetes would follow her wherever she went.

"She's just so interesting, and so pretty," Jess continued, "so I tried to figure out what academy she went to using her uniform crest. I found the train article instead."

Cooper knew this was when their mom would tell Jess that *she* was interesting and pretty, and she didn't need a fancy uniform or expensive school to be her amazing self. He tried to form the words, but it didn't work. Brothers didn't say that stuff. So instead he sat beside her and said, kindly, "Let's see what else we can find. What search terms did you use?"

"I searched 'bird and swords symbol,' but I had to scroll to, like, page twenty-eight before I found that newspaper picture."

"Well, maybe we can try it from the other direction: the schools. Type in 'private schools in Chicago.' Then we can look for a logo that matches hers."

Jess leaned ever so slightly closer to Cooper and said, "That was actually what I tried first, but I gave up when I saw there were four hundred and ten of them."

"Oh."

"And that doesn't even count the schools in the suburbs."

"Well, with two of us, it'll take half the time." Cooper navigated to the same search results on the iPad. "Some of these are preschools and kindergartens. We don't have to look at them." He scrolled further. "And here's a bunch that are high school only."

"How old do you think she is?"

"I don't know. Maybe twelve? Thirteen? I don't think she's in high school yet. Let's try searching 'private middle school Chicago,'" Cooper suggested. They both typed.

"Oh, that's better," Jess said. "Down to a hundred and seventy-six."

They agreed that Jess would start from the top of the list, linking to each home page and scanning for a school crest or symbol, and Cooper would start at the bottom. It proved to be a slow and tedious process.

"Wow, this whole middle school has only thirty-one students! That'd be weird," she said. "Yeesh. This one's like a prison."

Cooper looked at her screen and smiled. He hadn't hung out with Jess like this in a long time; it wasn't as terrible as he expected. They found a variety of school emblems, but most were predictably bland: outlines of church steeples; shields with a variety of books, mascots, and sporting equipment. A few had birds on them. But after one hundred and seventy-six links, none of them was exactly right. Jess shut the computer in frustration.

Searching for an image was more difficult than Cooper realized. Words are easy, but pictures—especially ones that are only in one's mind, without a specific title or name—are tougher.

"Maybe try falcon or raven or hawk instead of bird," Jess said.

Cooper did as she suggested, only to find a variety of coats of arms, a couple of video games, and ample images of the Hogwarts shield. Searching "two swords" took him deep into the world of tarot cards, and "hawk and two swords" brought up Renaissance festival pictures and a handful of very dated fantasy book covers with nearly naked women wielding knives. Adding "vigilantes" to the search didn't get them any further. The number of dead ends seemed endless.

"It's kind of amazing you found that article in the first place," Cooper said.

"Cooper!"

Both Cooper and Jess jumped at the sound of their mother's cry from the doorway of the room.

"I have been texting you for the last hour!" she continued. "Why didn't you send me your sister's sugar? And Jess, why are you still awake?"

Cooper glanced at the iPad screen. 9:56 p.m. His sister's bedtime was twenty-six minutes ago.

"Sorry, Mom. We—"

Mom didn't even pretend to listen; she took two strides and snatched both the iPad and laptop from their hands. She opened the computer, and the light from the screen uplit her face as it shifted from annoyance to surprise and then something else entirely.

"You're researching private schools?" she said in a quiet and deflated voice.

"Uhh . . ." Cooper watched awkwardly as his mom clicked back through screen after screen of smiling students in uniforms, performing science experiments and playing lacrosse. After a painfully long time, she closed the lid. "You both know we can't afford any of those schools."

What was Cooper supposed to say? That they weren't searching schools for the reason she suspected, that they were trying to solve a century-old mystery involving a dead British kid? Instead he muttered, "Sorry," again. It was all he had.

"Have you even checked your sugar, Jess?"

"Um . . . no."

Their mother tucked both of their screens under one arm and made a sweeping motion with the other. "Jess, go get your pj's on. I'll meet you in your room." She walked away to get Jess's supplies, shoulders slumped.

Jess and Cooper waited until Mom was out of earshot. "So what do we do now?" Jess whispered.

"Go to bed, I guess."

"You should try to talk to her."

"I don't think Mom wants anything to do with me right now."

"No, not Mom. That girl."

"Jess, it's ten o'clock."

Jess tipped her head back and moaned in frustration. "Not now, dum-dum. Tomorrow. You should ask her where she got that jacket."

"Why me?"

"Why not you?"

Sitting in his room doing internet searches was one thing. Actually talking to the creepy girl across the alley was another thing altogether. "This is your project, Jess, not mine."

"Jess!" their mother called from the hallway.

She jumped up and scooted off to her room.

Cooper changed into pajamas, and as he walked back toward his bed, he paused. He made sure Jess wasn't still in the hallway, then took a few side steps back to the window. Little mushroom lamps glimmered along the backyard path of the yellow house, leading from the alley to the back porch. Interior lights still warmed the downstairs windows, but upstairs, the curtains were drawn, and the lights were out. There would be no more surveillance tonight.

Cooper exhaled. As much as he hated to admit it, Jess was probably right: the easiest way to find out about the crest was to ask the girl herself. Searching for answers online could take forever, with no guarantee of finding anything at all.

But she was so *weird*.

Cooper jumped away from the window, however, when he heard his mother's voice in the hall right outside his room. "Let's go. Downstairs." It was followed by the sounds of footsteps trailing away toward the kitchen. The only reason Jess would go back downstairs after ten was because her blood sugar was too low and she needed more food.

Cooper knew that low blood sugar at bedtime meant a long and sleepless night for Jess and Mom: food every fifteen minutes until his sister's level was back where it should be; then Jess could sleep, but only for an hour until Mom woke her to recheck. If she slipped low again, they had to repeat the whole process. Possibly again and again and again, all with the hopes of avoiding a 911 call. They were always quiet outside Cooper's room, but that didn't mean he slept. Even though there was nothing he could do to help, sleeping somehow seemed rude.

Jess's half-woven friendship bracelet was still on Cooper's floor. He scooped it up, tiptoed into Jess's room, and put it on her pillow.

For a guy trying so hard not to care about others, this awful, hollow feeling in his gut sure *felt* like caring. Cooper crawled into bed without brushing his teeth and pulled his covers over his head.

7

The alarm had been blaring for two minutes before Cooper woke and smacked the off button, his head foggy and his eyes stinging. The night had been as long as he'd feared, his sister and Mom getting up countless times. Cooper woke with each, only to have his mind immediately launch into hyperdrive about his sister's blood-sugar levels, his dad's new baby, the train crash, and that crest. Sleep, so elusive for the past eight hours, now didn't want to let go of him.

And it now seemed it was the same for everyone else. Even after he'd showered, all was quiet. Cooper dressed and cracked the door to his mother's room.

"Mom?" he whispered.

The only response was a soft snore. He went to her bedside and gently shook her shoulder. "Mom."

She rolled slowly onto her back, eyes still closed, and mumbled something that sounded like "in a minute."

"Should I wake Jess up? It's after seven." He had to nudge her again before he got an answer.

"We're staying home today," she said, finally opening her eyes. "Last night was bad. I'll call school. Can you let the bus driver know?"

"Sure." Cooper felt the urge to apologize bubbling up like a belch, but he swallowed it back down. "Are you getting up?"

"Yeah, yeah. Give me a minute." Her eyelids sagged on the final word, and he left the room quietly.

Once in the kitchen, Cooper looked around for the iPad or laptop, wanting to research that crest a little more, but they were nowhere to be found. This hardly came as a surprise, as his mom frequently "hid" them in the bottom drawer of her bedside table, and he wasn't going back up there.

Instead, Cooper packed lunch and then sat down with a bowl of diabetic-approved Kellogg's All-Bran cereal. What he wouldn't give for a Lucky Charm. Just one. Or bacon. He nearly drooled at the thought. His dad loved meat—a good steak, thick pork chops, you name it—and Cooper had inherited his father's taste buds, much to his mother's dismay. He wondered if his dad was happier now that he could eat whatever he wanted without having to brush his teeth before kissing his new wife.

The sounds of his spoon against the bowl got louder with each bite.

Dad. New wife. New family. He had to get it out of his head.

Cooper dropped the spoon and pulled his dog-eared journal from his backpack. He opened to the next blank page and began dumping out his tangled mess of thoughts. It was something Cooper had started last year, when his seventh-grade teacher, Mrs. Wishingrad, began a section on keeping a journal. At first Cooper thought it was awful. He would turn in two or three short sentences on whatever topic Mrs. Wishingrad assigned. Five assignments into the unit, she asked Cooper to stay after class. He was certain he was in trouble, but instead she had him sit down beside her. In one hand she held his journal, in the other her phone.

"Cooper, you are a young man of few words," she began.

He proved her point by saying nothing.

"Have you ever heard of the phrase 'still waters run deep'?"

He gave a small head shake.

"I've been teaching for over thirty years, and in my experience, the kids who say the least often are the ones who have the most to say. I think you have a deep well of ideas, thoughts, and feelings under the surface."

Cooper felt his heart rate pick up. She had no idea what was under his surface. She didn't know anything about him, he wanted to say. But he just sat there, still.

"Sometimes," she continued, "getting all those ideas out is a challenge, because there are so darn many of them." She opened his journal to a clean page and swiped open her smartphone to a dictionary app. "I want you to ignore the journal assignment I gave the class for tonight. Instead, I want you to write five words."

"Five words?" That sounded easy, but Cooper wondered if he should feel insulted.

"That's right! But they have to be five *delicious words*." She wrote this heading at the top of the page in bright orange Sharpie.

"What's a delicious word?"

"It's a word that you didn't previously know, and one that you find particularly descriptive, or fun to say or write."

"Like what?"

"Like festoon!" she said with a flourish, and wrote the word at the top of the list.

Cooper's stern demeanor cracked slightly. He liked the

sound of the word, though he had no idea what it meant.

"It means to decorate something with many small objects." She pointed across the room. "As you can see, I have festooned the bulletin board with interesting facts and trivia." She typed the word into the dictionary app and scrolled to the bottom. "And here are tons of other delicious words that are similar: adorn, bedeck, fancify. Those are synonyms, or words that mean the same thing. But I want your words to have five different meanings, okay? And hey, look, I already did one for you! So all you have to do is write down four more delicious words, what they mean, and then read their synonyms."

"Okay . . . but why?"

"Because it's hard to say deep, complex things without deep, complex words to capture them, don't you think?"

Though Cooper initially thought the whole assignment was lame, he did as he was asked. His first list was: gild (to cover with a thin layer of gold), dawdle (to move or act slowly), gangly (tall, thin, and awkward), and malicious (showing a desire to cause harm to another person).

Mrs. Wishingrad continued to assign Cooper similar lists for the next few weeks. When Cooper forgot to erase a doodle of an angry little alien from the margins of his notebook, he worried his teacher would think he was wasting time; instead she encouraged him to draw more. So he did.

His illustrations consumed as much time and paper as his words. When the unit ended, most of his classmates' journals landed in the recycling bin, but Cooper's stayed tucked away in his bag.

He had filled many notebooks since. He wrote and drew, using the dictionary app to find words and definitions that read like they had been invented for him. Livid. Seething. Alienated. If such words existed, surely he wasn't alone in feeling them. Maybe he wasn't the only one whose father was a duplicitous, unconscionable, indefensible scoundrel.

Here, alone at the breakfast table, the familiar chaotic mix of words and drawings sprang from his pencil, a barely coherent, jumbled mishmash. He sketched a trail of tears swirling into a void, a young child begging a pitiless man to turn around, a disconsolate girl staring at an empty picture frame. This was all surrounded by flying springs, cogs, and watch shards. At one point, the tip of his pencil tore the paper as it practically sparked from the speed and pressure he lent the task. When, finally, his tap ran dry, he was able to put his pencil down.

Though the desire to break things always came first these days, it never calmed Cooper the way journaling and sketching did. At least for a little while, he would feel better.

He checked the clock and saw that he should already be on his way to the bus stop. He shoved the last bite of cereal into his mouth and dropped both the bowl and spoon into the sink with a clatter.

And there she was. Sitting in her backyard, uniform on, the girl looked at him through his kitchen window, the sun gleaming off the red stitching of the bird's eye on her jacket. Cooper decided to outstare her this time, to not so much as blink. His eyes started to burn, and he was sure he was going to win this battle of wills before the squeal of school bus brakes sent him running. He snatched his backpack, journal, and coat and flew out the front door.

Cooper scrambled aboard the bus with only one thought in mind: He was going to talk to her after school, no matter how strange she was. He was going to find out what that crest symbolized and where it came from.

8

For the first time in what seemed like forever, Cooper actually had plans after school. So, of course, every class dragged on forever. By the time Cooper walked into his house at the end of the day, he felt a little nauseated from both anticipation and fatigue.

He shouted for Jess and his mom as he came in the door and dropped his backpack, but there was no response. Though talking to the girl would be easier with no one else around, it worried him a bit that neither of them answered. That was when a buzzing sound against the hardwood floor prompted him to fish his phone out of his bag.

It was a text from his mother that read:

We are out running errands and grabbing groceries. Home in a couple hours. Love you.

Perfect.

Cooper grabbed an apple from the bowl on the kitchen counter and went to the sink to rinse it off. As the icy water trickled over his fingers, he looked out across the alley.

There she was. On her swing. In a refreshing twist, she wasn't staring at him, but rather staring straight ahead, motionless.

He should have been happy. It was the perfect opportunity to go over and talk to her. Instead, Cooper felt as chilled as his fingers.

There was something very wrong about her.

Appetite now gone, he put the apple back in the fruit bowl, wiped his hands on his pants, and slowly crossed to the back door. He took multiple deep breaths and swung the door open. It seemed colder outside than it had been moments before. Cooper moved onto the step and had to catch the knob as a gust of wind blew the door inward. He tugged it shut, crossed his arms against the chill, and walked across the alley toward the white picket fence. Squinting against the breeze, he yelled, "Hey!" over the creaking of branches overhead. The word sounded wobbly leaving his throat.

The girl, who could have been mistaken for a statue,

came to life. She pushed her heels into the earth and began swinging slightly, back and forth. Her thin, ungloved fingers wrapped gently around the braided rope that creaked and stretched with each pass.

"Kinda cold for swinging, huh?" Cooper said.

She slowly turned to look at him and shrugged.

"I'm Cooper."

He waited. *This, traditionally, is when you tell me your name,* he thought.

Nothing.

There, on her left breast pocket was the crest. Cooper could see the banner clutched in the talons of the bird with greater detail than he could last night, but he still couldn't make out the words from where he was standing.

He took one step closer and decided to wait out the awkward silence. Her shrug at least told Cooper that she could hear him; surely she would have to say something, eventually. He jammed his hands into his pockets, rocked on his heels, stared into her blue eyes, and nodded slowly. He waited.

And waited.

He soon realized he was the only one who seemed uncomfortable.

"And you are . . . ?" he finally blurted.

She tipped her head to the side, considering, before saying, "I'm Elena."

Her voice was a surprise, both in that she had one and in how warm it sounded. He had expected something thin and cold, like the rest of her.

"Oh! You *can* talk!" he said with a dramatic display of surprise.

"Of course I can." She stared so intently at Cooper that he had to turn away.

He rubbed the back of his neck. "Well, I've said hi to you before, and you've never said anything back."

She again responded with nothing but a stare.

He had never in his life spoken to anyone so uninterested in conversation. "Well, it's nice to finally meet you," he stuttered, sounding more like a dopey adult than himself. She was definitely strange, but she didn't seem as ominous or frightening now that they were talking. He shifted his feet and cleared his throat to try to reset his brain. "Hey, so . . . I wanted to ask you something."

She raised an eyebrow.

"I was curious. What school do you go to?"

For a millisecond, the air about her wavered. She cocked her head slightly to the other side, and there was a momentary crinkle around her eyes. But it passed quickly, and her placid expression returned. "Why do you ask?"

"Well, it's just that I haven't seen you at Eisenhower." He wanted to step forward again—to get a closer look at the words on the banner—but peering at that particular location of her body felt uniquely uncomfortable.

"That's because I don't go to Eisenhower," she said.

Cooper, again, waited for more, but it didn't come. "So . . ."

"I go to a small private school. I'm sure you've never heard of it."

"Oh, yeah? Which one?" He inched closer; squinting, he could read the entire banner. *Vigilantes Unum*. Was that Spanish? French? Did she go to some language immersion school? He averted his gaze and repeated the phrase in his mind to try to memorize it.

"Hey, Cooper!"

Cooper turned into the wind at the voice coming up the alley. It was Gus. He was walking toward them, shoulders hunched against the cold, a smile on his face.

"Gus!" Cooper said. It was good to see him again, but this wasn't the best timing.

"Whatcha doing?" Gus asked.

"Just talking," he said, tipping his head toward the swing. "Elena, this is Gus."

"I picked up on that," she said. Her voice had taken a distinctly cool turn.

73

"Hey," Gus said. He raised his hand in a friendly little wave that was not returned.

Cooper half hoped Gus had someplace to be and would simply walk on past, but instead he stopped expectantly. The three of them formed the points of an awkward triangle. Elena glared at Gus, as if he had interrupted something important, which might have made sense to Cooper if Gus had walked into an actual conversation, but Elena hardly seem interested in chatting anyway.

"So . . . what's up?" Cooper asked Gus.

"Going for a walk. My grandma says I need to get some exercise. I let her believe that's what I'm doing, but I really just like getting out of that house." He looked back and forth between Cooper and Elena. "You guys wanna do something?"

"Um . . ." Cooper looked at Elena and back at Gus. "Like what?"

"I don't know. We could play Low Budget?"

"What's that?" Cooper asked.

"It's a game where I make up an adventure, and you guys are the explorers. You tell me what you want to try to do, and I roll a die." He pulled a red piece of plastic from his pocket that appeared more like a ball than a cube. "One through twenty. If you get a high number, you succeed. A low number, you fail. In the end, it becomes, like, a whole story. It's basically a low-budget version of D&D. Hence the name."

"Maybe?" Cooper looked at Elena again, to see what she was thinking. This was not how he had expected this conversation to go, but he could find out more about her if they all hung out.

"I can't," Elena said.

Because you have a more pressing engagement with your swing? Cooper wondered. "Are you sure?" he asked.

"Quite. I'm not allowed to hang out with people I don't know," she said. "It's not safe."

Safe? Sure, none of them really knew each other that well, but he couldn't imagine anyone thinking he or Gus was dangerous. In fact, if there was anyone Cooper felt wary of, it was Elena.

"Maybe next time?" Gus said with a shrug, oblivious to the dark cloud hanging over Elena. He turned to Cooper. "The game doesn't really work with only one explorer. Do you want to hang out anyway? We could do something else."

Cooper wanted to talk more with Elena, given that he'd managed to extract exactly zero information from her other than her first name, which wasn't much help, and the fact that she went to a private school, which they pretty much already knew. But he still felt bad about what had happened with Gus at lunch the other day.

Cooper looked at Elena. She was staring at him with a steely gaze.

"Are you okay?" Cooper asked her.

She didn't respond. He didn't understand much about her, but it was very clear he wasn't going to get any more information from her today.

Cooper still staring at Elena, said, "Sure, Gus. Let's do something." He tried to take one last mental snapshot of the words on Elena's jacket. At the very least, he could Google them later. "Come on," he said, tipping his head toward his house. "This is my place."

"Oh, good," Gus said with a relieved grin. "It's cold out here."

"I'll see you later," Cooper said to Elena.

"Nice meeting you," Gus said.

Elena said nothing but got up and walked into her own home.

The warmth of the kitchen was a welcome reprieve from both the outdoors and Elena's chilly dismissal. Cooper jiggled his arms as if to shake off both. He slipped off his shoes and headed for the junk drawer, fishing out a small pad of paper and a pen. He scribbled down *Vigilantes Unum*, tore the page free, and stuffed it into his pocket. Then he moved to the snack drawer—something more than an apple was in order.

"So were you guys, like, breaking up or something?" Gus asked, peering over the lip of the drawer as well.

Cooper laughed. "What?"

"It was pretty tense out there. What's up with you two?"

"*Nothing* is up between us. Absolutely nothing." The only offerings left were his sister's gross Glucerna bars, which Cooper wasn't allowed to touch given how expensive they were, and a bag of corn chips. He grabbed the chips and some salsa from the fridge. It was no Snickers, but it was the best he had to offer. Gus smiled, and they both dug in.

"It was only tense," Cooper continued through a mouthful of chip, "because she's super weird. She moved in a few months ago, and that was actually the first time she's ever talked to me." He almost started to tell Gus about the mystery, but he thought better of it. Detailing the theory that Elena was wearing the mark of a long-dead kid was a bit much.

"Her place sure is . . ." It seemed like Gus was searching for the right word. "Nice? Like, way nicer than my grandma's house. But *she* seems kinda stuffy."

Cooper glanced through the window at the house and thought of Elena in her crisp pressed uniform. Then he looked at Gus's baggy sweatshirt and khakis with grass stains on the knees. "Yeah," Cooper said with a grin. "She does seem kinda *stuffy*."

They both stood by the counter, chewing. Cooper offered Gus something to drink, and then got him a glass of water. He vaguely recalled that he should offer something *to do* when a friend was over. It had been so long. "So, whatcha want to do?" he asked.

"I don't know. Is anyone else home?"

"No. My mom and sister are running errands."

Gus peered around the room, seeming to search for inspiration. "Do you have any comic books?"

"A couple." Cooper thought of the three partially ripped, ancient comics he might have under his bed. "I've also got the *Marvel Encyclopedia*. And a bunch of Far Side books." He kept quiet about his hoard of Garfield compilations. They were probably too old for that.

"I love The Far Side!"

"You do?" None of Cooper's friends thought those cartoons were funny. The Far Side was downright strange half the time, but Cooper had apparently inherited his father's sense of humor in addition to the books. "They're upstairs," Cooper said, and led the way up to his room.

"Cool," Gus said behind him. "I can't stay too long, or my grandma will think I got hit by a car."

Once they were in his room, Cooper handed Gus his favorite of the three massive tomes and grabbed his second favorite. They both plopped down on the floor and read, side by side. After a moment, Gus howled with laughter.

"Which one?" Cooper looked over.

"This one!"

Cooper knew it well. The picture showed three sad-faced cavemen in a circle, all showing "rock" with their fists in front of them. Below was the caption "Before scissors and paper."

"Dude is so weird, right?" Cooper said.

He scooted closer to Gus, and for half an hour, they both read the book in Gus's lap, cracking up and pointing at their favorites. They took turns explaining the cartoons that the other didn't get. They shrugged and skipped the ones neither of them understood.

"My dad said those'll make more sense when I get older," Cooper said.

"Sounds like my dad." Gus's voice dropped to a deep bass, and he said, "'Son, there are things you're too young to understand,' like I'm three years old or something. I get *way* more than he or my mom thinks."

Cooper nodded. "It's crazy what parents think we don't understand, right? Like, when my parents told us they were getting divorced, they started by saying, 'We know this is going to come as a surprise.' I had a lot of feelings about it, but by that point surprise was *not* one of them." Cooper's eyes burned at the memory, and he clenched his jaw as he finished speaking. He hated the memory of that day because he had still been slightly hopeful, still innocent of all that was yet to come. He reached over and flipped to the next page of his Far Side book, but he did it too hard and tore the bottom edge.

Gus fell quiet. He stared intently at the cartoons, his own eyes a little shinier than they had been a moment earlier. Cooper's anger fell away, and he felt like kicking himself. Why had he brought up divorce? He'd had years to deal with the disintegration of his parents' marriage, but Gus was only at the beginning of that particular terrible rollercoaster ride.

Cooper managed a slight "I didn't mean to . . ."

"It's okay," Gus murmured. "It's just . . . I don't know. My parents have separated before but always managed to work things out. But they've never sent me away. I keep hoping, but the longer I'm here, the less I think it's going to be okay."

Cooper wanted to say something, to fill the silence that followed, but stating everything would be fine felt like a lie. He could offer no such assurances, and he wasn't going to lie to Gus again.

Gus instead spoke next. "So, how long has it been for you?"

"Three years since it was final." The total time of misery was longer, but Cooper didn't see the point in going into more detail.

Gus nodded for a moment before saying, "Well, you've made it through. It's not like my parents splitting up will kill me, right?"

Cooper was pretty sure no one should look at him as a role model in divorce survival. He picked at a hole in his sock, pulling an elastic thread so taut it snapped. "Maybe?" he said.

"Does it get easier?"

"It gets . . . different."

Cooper had never wanted to talk about his parents' divorce with anyone his age before. But somehow, with Gus, it was okay. Cooper didn't know if it was because Gus was going through the same thing, or the fact that Gus hadn't witnessed the very public and embarrassing exposure of Cooper's father's lies. There was a sort of relief in talking to someone with shared struggles, but it was also like scratching a poison-ivy rash—satisfying, but painful at the same time. Whatever he felt, though, it was nice to feel slightly less alone.

An idea sprouted in Cooper's brain. "Do you want to do something a little weird?" he asked with a mischievous smile.

Gus screwed up his mouth, tentatively. "Sure?"

"Call your grandma," Cooper said, taking the Far Side book and tossing it onto the bed. "You need to tell her you're going to be out for a while."

9

It took Cooper and Gus twenty minutes to walk to their destination. The highway bridge wasn't much to look at, with its exposed rebar, rust-stained cracks, and graffiti-marred surfaces, but maybe that was part of why it was Cooper's favorite place in the whole world. It was a damaged, rundown, neglected old thing just trying to do its job. As he guided Gus onto the pedestrian path, he kicked a large chunk of the crumbling sidewalk cement ahead of them. Gus kicked it in turn, and they traded kicks back and forth as their ears filled with the sound of the rumbling river below. Traffic hummed directly beside them, only a concrete barrier away. Cooper had started coming here last year, on his own. It was one of the few places in the city that was out in the open, but where no one (save the people in the speeding cars) ever came. And Cooper had never shared it—not this way, at least—with anyone.

"We're here," he announced with a flourish at the center of the bridge.

Gus halted beside him, peering at the river sixty feet below and the downtown buildings just past the other end of the bridge. He gave Cooper a quizzical look. "Here" didn't seem like anywhere in particular.

"Now, what I am going to show you is a little strange, but I've found it helps a lot."

"Okay?" Gus said curiously.

Cooper put a foot on the outer curb, grabbed the cool metal railing, and leaned his weight back as far back as he could. Then, with all the force he could muster, he yanked himself forward, bent his waist over the rail, and screamed. He yelled with all he had in him, emptying his chest until it burned, before taking another gulp of air to do it all over again.

After his third or fourth bellow, he turned to a stunned Gus and grinned. "Go on! Try it."

Gus didn't move at all, but a blush of embarrassment bloomed on his face.

"Seriously!" Cooper laughed. The cars kept whizzing

past. "No one cares. Give it a go. I swear, it helps."

"Just . . . scream?"

"Yup. Just scream."

Slowly, cautiously, Gus took a breath. He then released a sad little yelp that made Cooper laugh even harder.

"No, you weirdo! Not like that. Like this!" And again, Cooper released a shriek like he was being stabbed. When he finished, he waved an arm to Gus, giving him the floor.

Gus smiled, grabbed the railing, inhaled with all he had, and bellowed out over the river and the city beyond. His voice blended with the sounds of squeaky brakes, rushing water, and ever-present car horns. It broke through the river mist and engine exhaust—a wild animal released from its pen—before dissolving away. Then he did it again.

After he'd done it four or five more times, Gus turned to Cooper. He seemed a little lighter, and his cheeks had a healthy flush in them. Cooper gave him an inquiring glance, one eyebrow up.

Gus nodded.

Together they leaned back, their bodies making forty-five-degree angles with the sidewalk, before hoisting themselves in sync toward the rail.

They wailed at the world together. They howled again and again, in unison, but not one driver turned to look at two young boys screaming their pain away. Cooper screamed away ugly, amorphous things that he didn't have the courage to put in his journal: *I'm not worth sticking around for. Dad never cared about me. It's all my fault.*

Cooper always felt a release after he roared like this, but this time, with Gus, something wholly unexpected happened. Their final howl ended in panting laughter.

"Better?" Cooper asked when he finally caught his breath, his voice ragged and torn.

"Yeah," Gus said, leaning against the railing, spent but smiling. "For sure. I think I need a lozenge."

"A *lozenge*? You really *do* live with an eighty-year-old woman!"

Gus punched Cooper in the arm.

Two semi trucks, one from each direction, barreled across the bridge, passing the boys at the exact same time. It caused such a jarring shudder beneath their feet that Gus gripped the handrail with both hands and let out a small yelp. Cooper, in contrast, assumed a surfer's stance.

Once the roar of the engines passed, Gus said, "Okay, that was terrifying! Is this thing made of aluminum foil?"

Cooper jiggled an extended pinkie and thumb. "It's all part of the bridge-screaming experience. This bridge is crazy old; they keep talking about replacing it, but nothing ever happens. You should feel this thing shake when there's even more traffic. You'd swear the whole thing was going to fall down."

"I'm gonna pass."

Now it was Cooper's turn to imitate his friend's frightened face. He reenacted the scared expression Gus had made when discussing his grandmother at lunch that first day. Again, they both ended up in giggles. Ultimately, they looked out over the city, elbows on the railing, one foot on the curb, sharing a quiet moment.

Finally Gus said, "It's really pretty from here."

"Right?" This was Cooper's favorite view of downtown, with its innumerable skyscrapers made of stone, steel, and glass, showcasing over a century of architectural history all from one spot. On a clear day, the blue hues of the river and sky reflected off the thousands of windows. It was beautiful and so different from his neighborhood just a few minutes away, with its many tired and worn houses. His street was like a bad dream the city had forgotten.

He pointed out his favorite buildings to Gus: the corncob-shaped Marina City, the undulating wavy surface of Aqua, and the Aon building, with its stark white lines that reminded him of a tower fan. And of course, there was the pride of Chicago in the distance, the second-tallest building in the United States: the Sears tower. Cooper knew it wasn't called that anymore, but his parents had never called it Willis Tower, so neither did he.

There was something comforting about being so small in comparison to everything around them, a city teeming with people and lives and stories. In these moments, Cooper felt like maybe his small part of it all would be manageable in the end, somehow.

"Did you know they dye the river green for St. Patrick's Day every year?" Cooper asked.

"What?" Gus said. "How is that even possible?"

"They have some secret-formula powder they put in the water. It only lasts a few hours, but it's pretty cool. We can come down here in March and see."

"Yeah, maybe . . . ," Gus said, and Cooper understood his hesitation. March was months away. Gus's situation might be very different by then.

"So," Cooper said, "when do you think you'll know what's up at home? With your mom and dad?"

"Not sure. Don't ask questions you don't want the answers to, you know?"

Cooper nodded. Then, before he even knew the words were coming, Cooper blurted, "I lied to you."

Gus appeared taken aback by this out-of-the-blue admission. "What?"

"I lied to you. About my dad. He's not a marine."

Gus turned his gaze back out over the water, seeming to measure how to respond.

"I told you that because the truth's . . . because it's embarrassing. He actually lives in San Diego. He's a cardiologist. "

"Like a heart doctor?" Gus looked at Cooper askance with a laugh. "That doesn't seem very embarrassing."

Cooper didn't entirely understand why he was telling Gus this now. He hadn't intended to turn the conversation to his father. "I guess I thought that, when your dad's a marine, you don't have to explain why you never see him."

"Oh," Gus said quietly. "But California . . . that's got to be cool."

"I wouldn't know."

"Seriously?"

"Seriously. I've never been."

"I thought you said your parents divorced three years ago."

"I did, but he's never invited me. I guess he just . . . doesn't want to see me."

There it was. He'd said it.

"Whoa. That's so . . ." But Gus didn't finish. There was no good finish to that sentence. "Man, I'm sorry."

"Yeah. Me too."

"If it makes you feel any better, I've wanted to lie about my parents, too. Only I never came up with anything as cool as the marines."

Cooper laughed, relieved that Gus wasn't put off by what he'd told him. "Well, if you're gonna be a liar, I guess it's best to be a good liar."

Gus looked him straight in the eye. "Thanks for telling me."

Cooper nodded. He wanted to thank Gus for being the kind of person to whom he *could* tell the truth, but he didn't have the right words for it. Instead, he looked out again over the city.

"And thanks for bringing me down here," Gus said. "I feel a lot better."

"Yeah." Cooper nodded. "Me too."

"Hey, Coop!" his mom called when she saw him and Gus coming down the alley. "Come help carry groceries, please."

Gus checked his watch. "I should get home."

"What? You don't want to help with groceries?" Cooper teased.

"Nope! See ya tomorrow?"

"Yeah. Later."

Gus gave all the Stewarts a slight wave as he passed their

driveway and continued down the alley in the direction of Ms. Dreadful's house.

"Isn't that the guy who sits up with the kindergartners on the bus?" Jess asked as their mom took her bags inside.

"Are you actually making a new friend?" she said with mock surprise.

"I'm not a monster, you know."

Jess tipped her chin down and stared at him through heavy lids.

"He's nice," Cooper said with a shrug.

"It wasn't *his* niceness I was worried about."

They walked into the house, and something glass clattered ominously within one of Jess's bags as she set it on the counter. Cooper looked in the bag to see a jar of pickles on its side, but not broken. "How are you feeling?"

"Fine. Just tired."

Cooper moved closer to Jess to get a stealth sniff. No Juicy Fruit.

"Stop sniffing me," Jess said, skirting away from him. "I told you, I'm fine."

"Just checking."

"Jess, help me put things away," their mother said, unpacking her own bag. "And Cooper, I think there are still a few more bags in the car."

"Got it." Cooper slid past his mom and headed back outside. Hands full with the last of the bags, he pressed the garage-door button with his elbow and maneuvered out of the garage carefully. He looked at Elena's empty yard, wondering if maybe she'd be around later for another attempt at conversation.

As he stood wondering, Elena's house suddenly went dark. Every light, as if all on a giant master switch, went out at once.

Cooper froze. With a quick glance, he confirmed every other house down the alley was still lit. Maybe the yellow house had blown a fuse? Or . . . all the fuses? At the same time? As goose bumps rose on his arms, he ran up the steps a little faster than usual and kicked the door shut behind him.

10

"Hey, easy with the door!"

"Sorry, Mom." Cooper lugged the last bags to the counter and began to unload them. He could practically feel the piece of paper he'd jotted on earlier in his pocket. The sooner they finished putting away the groceries, the sooner he could search for whatever *Vigilantes whatever-it-was* meant.

"Did you pick up your sister's homework from the office?"

"Yeah, it's in my backpack." *Like always.*

"Sweetie, you can be done here. Go start on your schoolwork."

Cooper suppressed his desire to roll his eyes. Jess didn't have to go to school. She didn't have to finish putting away the groceries. Maybe she would like him to do her homework for her too. He didn't realize he'd closed the cupboard with too much force until he heard the wineglasses on the adjoining shelves shudder against each other.

"Cooper?" his mom said, head tipped.

"Sorry," he mumbled. "Can I go work on homework too?"

His mother sighed. "I assumed you were already done since you were out running around the neighborhood." She perused all the food still on the counter, then waved a hand at him. "Okay. Go. But please fold these bags and put them away first."

Cooper did as he was asked, grabbed his backpack, and bounded up the stairs.

"Dinner will be ready soon!" his mom called after him.

Out of guilt, he did tend to some schoolwork but was done with his math in seven minutes flat. He then pushed back on two chair legs to straighten his body out and fish the small piece of paper from his pocket, almost tipping over backward in the process.

"*Vigilantes Unum*," he read aloud, flattening the crumpled wad against his desk to read it better. He already knew what a vigilante was, but unum? He knew he'd heard that word somewhere before, but he couldn't recall where.

Jess peeked around Cooper's bedroom door, iPad in hand. "Did you talk to her?"

"Yeah, I actually did."

A huge grin blossomed on her face. "Really?"

He waved for her to come in and close the door. "Her name's Elena, but she didn't really tell me much before Gus came by. Just that she goes to a private school." He grabbed the piece of paper from his desk and handed it to her. "That's what the banner on her crest says. Do you know what 'unum' means?"

Jess furrowed her brow as she took it. "You mean like in 'e pluribus unum'?"

Cooper snapped his fingers. "Of course! That's where I've heard it!" He picked a dime out of a cup of change that sat on the corner of his desk. The Latin words gleamed up at him from between the torch and the branches on the back of the coin.

"Out of many, one," Jess said, standing a bit taller. "I did that project in fourth grade on U.S. currency, remember?"

"So, like Vigilante Number One? Punisher Numero Uno?" Cooper grimaced. He held his hand out for the iPad and did a Google image search using "Vigilantes Unum" as his search term. This time, only a small number of relevant images came up.

"That's it, right?" Jess said, pointing.

Under her finger was an exact match of the crest, and this time it was a detailed photograph. The image was more than the crest by itself: it was a picture of a V-neck T-shirt with the crest stitched onto the chest pocket. The shirt looked like it had been worn into battle. Cooper guessed the fabric had been white at one time, but it was difficult to say with all the dirt and rust-colored stains that covered it. There were tears in the fabric, and it was hopelessly wrinkled despite it being flattened out on a white table for the picture. A pencil was barely visible at the corner of the photo, offering some perspective on size.

The garment appeared small enough to fit Jess.

Cooper clicked the thumbnail and waited to be linked to the photograph's source page, excitement brewing in his chest. But then both he and Jess sagged at what came up.

"What is that? Chinese?" she asked.

"I have no idea."

The iPad screen was filled with the front page of an Asian newspaper. Jess and Cooper couldn't read it, but they didn't need to to understand what was being reported. A photograph dominated the space above the fold, showing a building in ruins. Two five-story bright pink walls still stood facing each other, bracketing a pile of rubble like two lonely and useless sides of a bookcase whose shelves had collapsed. Rebar dangled from the walls' edges like gnarled witch's fingers. Between them, piles of twisted metal and crumbled cement lay under a cloud of dust.

"Whoa," Jess said. "Is that from, like, an earthquake or something?"

Cooper scrolled down to a collection of smaller pictures at the bottom of the newspaper's front page. In addition to the dirty T-shirt, there were multiple damaged items displayed: a bent wedding ring, a cracked Mickey Mouse wristwatch, a dusty pair of purple women's designer boots.

"We have to find something about this in English." Cooper started typing again in the images search bar. "How many destroyed buildings can there be that look like they were painted with Pepto-Bismol?" But he didn't find anything related when he searched "pink building bomb."

"Try 'pink building earthquake,'" Jess suggested.

Nothing.

On his third try, using "pink building collapse," the search returned a seemingly endless stream of images of the building from the newspaper article, from every possible angle. Before he could scroll down, Jess reached over his shoulder and tapped ALL at the top of the Google search, bringing them results that included text as well as images.

The top link was a *New York Examiner* article from 1995. The headline read:

South Korean Department Store Collapses

Cooper tapped the link.

SEOUL, South Korea, Friday, June 30—Rescue workers dug for hours in the ruins of the Sampoong shopping mall today, hoping to find survivors in the rubble of the five-story building, which collapsed June 29.

Witnesses described how the catastrophe occurred, starting from the top down, each layer crushing the floor beneath.

Park Cho told KBS-TV he was on the ground floor Thursday before the collapse. "I felt a terrible quake, and then people began racing down from the upper floors." The owner of a top-floor restaurant told MBC-TV that he had reported a crack in his kitchen floor to store officials earlier in the day, but states he was reassured that it was not of concern and told to remain open.

Police now say the operators of the complex had known for hours that the top floor was failing but took no action. They were not in the mall at the time of the accident.

When the top floor finally did give way, it took only twenty seconds for the entire building to collapse.

"Wait. What?" Jess said. "It just *fell down*? That's not even possible. How does a building fall down?"

Cooper went back and linked to another article dated six months later. He skimmed down to a section that read:

Investigators have found ample evidence that Sampoong Mall was constructed with substandard cement and steel, and the roof was of insufficient strength to support the heating and cooling systems placed atop it.

Today, the owner of the mall, who had expressly ordered the building built with these specifications to maximize profit, was sentenced to ten years in prison for criminal negligence. Five civil servants have also been arrested on bribery and corruption charges for allowing the building to operate despite not meeting safety standards.

The collapse, which occurred in June of this year, left 937 people injured and more than five hundred dead.

"Five hundred!" Jess gasped.

"Oh no," Cooper whispered. He felt a trapdoor give way in his gut, that feeling of freefall at the beginning of a roller coaster's descent. The scope of this tragedy was not the cause, however. He hit the back button of the browser multiple times, returning to the site he now suspected was written in Korean. "Look down here, at the bottom, Jess. These pictures."

The siblings exchanged a heavy glance.

"These must all be items found on people who were in that building," Cooper said. "They are all super distinctive, right?" He pointed at the Mickey Mouse watch and the unique pair of boots, not wanting to touch the crest. "I think they put these things in the newspaper because they needed the public's help."

Jess's eyebrows drew so close, they were like one woolly caterpillar. "What are you saying?"

"I'm saying the two times we've found this symbol so far . . . I think the wearer ended up dead."

"And unidentified," Jess added softly. They both sat back and stared at each other, challenging the other to say something that made sense. Jess finally spoke. "So, what? Elena's in danger?"

"I . . . I don't know about that," Cooper said. "I mean, wherever she goes to school, there have to be dozens of other people wearing that symbol, right? Kids, teachers? And we know the symbol has been around as long as that train accident in 1928, so that's like hundreds, maybe thousands of people who have worn it over the years."

"You mean the school no one can find?"

Cooper's mouth went dry, and he found it nearly impossible to swallow. Both of them turned their heads and peered out the window toward Elena's darkened house.

"Dinner!" their mother called from downstairs.

"Okay," Jess said quietly to Cooper. "Maybe you're right, maybe Elena isn't in any danger, but don't you think we should at least go tell her about these articles? I mean, I'd want to know if I was wearing something that was tied to two tragedies like this."

"Guys! Did you hear me?" came another call from the kitchen.

"Yeah, Mom! We're coming," Jess yelled back.

They both rose slowly, still staring out the window. Cooper didn't know about Jess, but he suddenly didn't have much of an appetite.

11

Jess was right. They had to talk to Elena.

They at least had to tell her what they'd found online, tell her they had reason to worry she might be in harm's way, as crazy as that sounded. At the same time, they needed to know what she knew about the history of the crest, her school, or the past victims. She wasn't someone who was all that into sharing, but maybe the articles they'd found would convince her. She might hold the key to deciphering what was turning into a very ominous puzzle.

But first, dinner.

Cooper pushed his stir-fry and rice around the plate,

trying to make it look like he had eaten enough to be excused. Normally, Jess would have been chatting away with their mom, but she too was focused on her plate.

"You two okay?" Mom asked. She probably assumed they'd been fighting, a historically solid bet.

They looked at each other and then nodded.

Mom chewed slowly, appraising both of them. "Okay. So what's up?"

"Nothing," Cooper said. But Mom wasn't looking at him; she was staring at his sister. Jess never kept anything from her.

Jess shrank a little before putting a limp chunk of broccoli in her mouth and muttering, "Nothing, Mom."

Though she clearly wasn't buying it, their mother at least let it go. "You both have laundry to fold after dinner. And Cooper, I want to see your planner and your *finished* homework before bed. And not only the stuff that's due tomorrow—I'd like to see the progress on your essay that's due next week. How's that coming along?"

Just like that, Cooper's entire evening was gone. He hadn't done any work on the essay, a fact his mother already seemed to know. Any chance of slipping out to talk to Elena tonight vanished before his eyes. He convinced himself that it was a good thing, that he now had more time to plan for their conversation.

After lights-out that night, Cooper stared up at his darkened ceiling until well after midnight.

The next day, Cooper waved at Gus from where he was sitting with Zack when Gus boarded. Though Gus didn't sit any closer, he did give a little wave back, and smiled.

At noon, Cooper was on his way to the cafeteria when he slowed slightly while passing by Mrs. Wishingrad's old room. She had retired last year, and seeing her room *festooned* with the decor of some other teacher still bummed Cooper out. But today, even though it was lunchtime, there was someone in there. Alone.

Cooper poked his head in the doorway. "Gus?"

"Oh, hey, Coop," Gus said with a start. "Sorry. Cooper."

"That's okay. You can call me Coop. Are you studying or something?"

"Um . . ." Gus looked around, as if unsure he was allowed to be in here. "Yes?" He then shook his head. "No. Not really."

"Want company?"

"Sure!"

Cooper dragged a desk closer to Gus's and sat, unpacking his lunch. He opened a Snickers, bent it, and placed half on Gus's desk. "So, what's up?"

"Just living, you know."

"What'd you end up doing last night?"

"Homework. Otherwise known as hiding from my grandma. You?"

There was no way to go into the details of what he and Jess had found out about the crest and the accidents. He would sound like a kook if he started sharing their rather fantastical conspiracy theories without more concrete information. "Pretty much the same, but my mom wouldn't leave me alone."

"Why aren't you in the cafeteria?" Gus asked. "Isn't Zack going to wonder where you are?"

Cooper shook off the suggestion. "Nah. Zack's pretty used to me not showing up for things. He knows that sometimes I need to be alone."

"If he comes by, I'll totally hide." Gus pretended to see if there was room in his brown paper bag.

Cooper gave Gus a small laugh. "It's weird. Zack and I used to be so tight. I'd go over to his house all the time, especially when my parents were fighting. But after my dad left, it was like he knew too much. It got hard to be around him. I don't know . . . that probably doesn't make much sense."

Gus took a bite of Snickers.

Cooper weighed telling Gus about *that* night. About what had happened right before his dad left for good, the event that had created the horrifying memory that now stood like a ghost between Cooper and Zack every time they were together. On one hand, it was nice that Gus didn't know exactly what had happened with his dad. On the other, it seemed like he might be one person who could understand. Who wouldn't look away from it, or pretend it hadn't happened.

Because Gus knew what it was like to feel forgotten. Unseen.

Gus stayed quiet and took another bite of his lunch. He didn't seem to be waiting on, or pressuring, Cooper to say more. It was more like he was comfortable hanging out in whatever space Cooper needed while deciding how to proceed.

"So this thing happened, back when Zack and I were nine. My mom was out of town for a few weeks because my grandma had fallen and broken her hip, so my dad had to do everything while she was gone. Neighbors and friends helped out with me and Jess when my dad was at work, and there was this one Friday my dad had to work late and couldn't take care of us. I was spending the night at Zack's, and Jess was at some friend's house."

Cooper could almost feel the beautiful spring night as he remembered it. It had been one of those first warm days of the year, when parents insist their kids take a jacket to school even though the kids know they don't need it. Zack and Cooper had rolled off the bus together and, after a short Nerf battle in the yard, had gone inside to get ready.

"We had a baseball game that afternoon. I hit my only double ever. Zack's dad cheered extra loud since my dad wasn't there, which was nice of him, I guess. After the game, we celebrated at Dairy Queen and then decided to go to a movie. I really wished my dad hadn't been stuck at work, because he used to love movies." Cooper started to feel ill. His father always talked about how, when Cooper got older, he would share some of his favorite movies with him. He called them "films"—*The Godfather, Casablanca, Citizen Kane*.

Gus shifted in his seat, but only in a way that showed he was listening, not fidgety.

"So when the movie was over, we were walking out of the theater, Zack and I quoting our favorite lines and cracking each other up. I don't think his dad liked the movie very much, but even he was laughing with us. I was still laughing when, down the long hallway, I saw this guy who looked *exactly* like my dad. My first thought, seriously, was how crazy it was that two men could look so similar."

Cooper didn't need to finish the story. It was obvious how this ended. But he wanted to. Gus was still listening, not taking his eyes off Cooper, and now that he was in the middle of it, Cooper decided he *needed* Gus to hear it.

"So then this guy I'm looking at puts his hand through his hair exactly the same way my dad did. And I'm thinking, *Wow! What are the chances?* And then he coughs, covering his mouth with a hand that has a gold wedding band that looks *just like* my dad's. And then I was like, *Hey! Why is this man wearing my dad's jacket?*"

"Oh, man," Gus sighed.

"And Zack and his dad are both looking at me, then looking at him, then looking at me. And all these other people are walking around us. And at that point I decided my dad must be here to find me, like there's been an emergency or something. But then I watched him throw away a popcorn bag and take a last long slurp from his soda. He'd just been there seeing a movie."

Cooper paused for a moment. Retelling his father's first of so many lies still struck Cooper with a sickening force.

Gus was now leaning forward on his desk. "Did he see you?"

"Oh yeah. When he turned around to leave, he saw me standing there like an idiot, with my mouth gaping open. We all stood there for what felt like hours. Then he just turned and walked out the door, like he hadn't seen me at all."

Gus gently shook his head.

"So we left too. And I stayed at Zack's for the night, exactly like we'd planned, across the street from my own bed. It was so pathetic. I was the kid whose own dad didn't even want him around. Zack tried to cheer me up, we played video games all night and his dad made us popcorn and stuff, but . . ."

"What happened the next time you saw your dad?"

"The next morning, when I came home, I walked in and he was sitting at the kitchen table. He just looked at me over his coffee and said, 'You know, taking care of you and your sister is harder than you think.' Like, riiiiight. Got it. It's all our fault."

"Dude. What did your mom say when you told her?"

Cooper snorted. "You are the only person I've ever told that story to. And, like, I know he means well, but after that night, Zack's dad appointed himself my official dad understudy, or something. He hollers for me to 'come over to throw a ball around' with him and Zack or asks me to go out to dinner with them. He even invited me on a fishing weekend with him and Zack and Zack's uncle. But I barely go over there at all anymore." Being in the Tyson home felt like Cooper was standing on the dining-room table in his underwear, exposed and on display for all to see, like some diorama in a Museum of Unnatural Family History.

Cooper had worried he might feel like that now too,

after telling Gus about what had happened. That story was a stinking pile of personal garbage, something to put down and run away from. But Gus didn't seem to mind. He didn't even flinch.

As the bell rang for fifth hour, Cooper expected a wave of extreme self-consciousness and regret to crash over him, but it never arrived. Instead both he and Gus packed up their lunches in a comfortable quiet, leaving the story Cooper had told hanging in the air between them.

And it was okay.

Gus put a hand on Cooper's shoulder as they walked out of the room, and together they headed off toward their next classes.

12

The Friday-afternoon bus was as loud and raucous as ever, but Jess and Cooper sat together silently. Unlike every other kid, they weren't big fans of Fridays. The Stewart family tradition of Friday movie night—pizza, four people under a too-small blanket on the couch, and popcorn at the halfway point—used to be the best part of every week. It had been a regular reassurance that even as a hurricane seemed to be gaining strength all around them, there was calm at its core.

But then the hurricane had shifted and blown it all away.

Mom had tried to keep Friday movie night going after Dad left, but soon she had needed the job at the arts center.

These days, Jess made PB&Js for the two of them (easy on the J for her) and begged Cooper to watch something with her under that same blanket, which felt huge now. Half the time he just said no, retreating to his room to journal or watch YouTube; the other half he ended up on the couch, arguing with Jess about what to watch before begrudgingly settling on *Survivor* reruns for the thousandth time. They certainly never watched "films."

Tonight, however, they had a different plan in mind: talk to Elena. A plan they were both excited about.

However, to both Cooper and Jess's surprise, their mother was home when they got off the bus, saying she had requested the night off from her pottery class because "There's too much to do here at the house."

From the minute he and Jess got home, Mom had them working. It was as if she was trying to do some family bonding through intense manual labor. The list of fall chores she had prepared kept Jess and Cooper hustling not just that afternoon, but all weekend: raking, sweeping out the garage, clearing their drawers of clothes to give away. Shrub pruning, bulb planting, and mulch spreading.

And Elena sat perched on her swing, watching it all.

By Sunday evening, however, the to-do list was finally complete. And as they washed and dried the dinner dishes, and the sun sank low toward the horizon, Cooper and Jess hatched a plan: Cooper would go over and talk to Elena while Jess stayed home to keep their mom distracted over a game of cards.

Right as he was about to slip out the back door, his mother came back into the kitchen for a glass of water.

"Where are you going?"

"Um . . ." He remembered how Jess had made fun of him when she caught him looking over at Elena's bedroom through his telescope. The last thing he needed his mom thinking was that he had a crush on the girl next door. "I'm, uh, going to go write in my journal. Out back."

"Wouldn't you need your journal then?" she asked with a raised eyebrow.

"Ha! Yeah. Right." Cooper ran to his room, giving Jess an annoyed glare where she sat guiltily holding her cards in the living room, and was back in no time flat.

"It's too dark out there, bud. Why don't you work in here instead?"

"I can still see fine, Mom." Cooper grabbed a pencil from her desk. "The moon's super bright."

"Well, come back in if you're straining your eyes. You don't want to give yourself a headache."

"Whatever, Mom," Cooper said, and hurried outside.

Of course, now, Elena's swing was empty—it swayed gently back and forth in the brisk evening breeze—but

Cooper had been waiting all weekend to talk to her, and he wasn't going to miss this chance. He tossed his journal on top of the trash-can lid beside him, took a deep breath, and hurried to the edge of his backyard. He stood with his toes on his own property line, staring up at the yellow house. It seemed larger now, more imposing. Most of the lights were on inside, and woodsmoke rose from the chimney. The aroma was welcoming, like the house was inviting Cooper to come over and stay awhile.

That was when the house flickered.

Like a digital glitch interrupting a streaming video, so brief you aren't sure if it even happened, the entirety of the home shifted and blinked; the yellow siding flashed the brown of old paint and dirt; the white window frames were replaced by gaping holes of darkness. Cooper's pulse sped up as he blinked and rubbed his eyes.

What was . . . ?

He looked again. Butter yellow. Sparkling glass. Green grass.

Was he losing his mind? A frigid gust of wind that held the promise of winter propelled him forward. He shoved his hands in his pockets, elbows locked against his sides, took a deep breath, and stepped into the alleyway.

The blare of a car horn pierced the air. Cooper leaped

back as his neighbor, Mr. Evans, skidded his Suburban to a halt.

"Cooper!" he said, rolling down his window. "I'm sorry! I saw you there, but I didn't think you were going to step in front of me like that."

Mr. Evans's words sounded muffled in Cooper's ears, blocked by the blood flooding his eardrums. "Sorry," Cooper said. "I didn't see you."

Mr. Evans tipped his head, as if to ask how Cooper could possibly miss the headlights of his huge vehicle in an alley that was hardly wider than the car itself. But what he said was, "My fault, kiddo. I should have been going slower."

Cooper took another step back as Mr. Evans crawled past with a wave and turned into his own garage, twenty feet away. Something small and black shot past Cooper's feet, startling him yet again, but it was only Mr. Evans's cat, Panther, darting home at the sound of his meal provider's arrival. Cooper watched the garage door close and tried to slow his breathing, before—with a side-to-side look this time—he stepped forward again.

The gate latch of Elena's picket fence was painfully cold. Maybe this was a stupid idea. Had he really studied that T-shirt from the Korean newspaper closely enough? Maybe the crest was slightly different. Or even if it was the same, it didn't necessarily mean anything. Maybe someone who'd gone to Elena's school back in the nineties had visited Korea and was unfortunately killed in the accident. He turned toward his own home, about to walk back across the alley.

But there was Jess, peering out the kitchen window at him. She smiled and gave him a double thumbs-up.

Cooper gave her a weak one in return. He turned, pushed the gate open, and walked into Elena's yard.

He slid slightly on a blanket of wet leaves atop the path of stepping-stones. His hands shot out to steady himself, as if he was a child taking his first step onto an ice rink in skates. The damp soil on both sides of the path gave off an odor of mushrooms and decay. The latch clicked shut behind him.

Cooper slowly stood up straighter and wondered if maybe he should walk around to the front door and knock. Was it too presumptuous to come through their backyard?

Well, he thought, *we're friends now, right? We know each other's names. We had a conversation. Most of one, anyway.*

He walked between the two rows of landscaping lights bracketing the path, through the yard, and up to the white-washed porch. The first wooden step groaned slightly at Cooper's weight. He chewed on the inside of his bottom lip and crept up onto the deck. With the sense that he was pulling a Band-Aid off much too slowly, Cooper picked up his pace.

With each step toward the door, the stale autumn scents in the yard were pleasantly replaced by an aroma of pumpkin, cinnamon, and cloves. Cooper stood with his fist raised for a few seconds before finally rapping on the wooden edge of the screen door. But instead of a solid, crisp knock, the wood released only a quiet, damp thud.

When no one answered, Cooper scanned for a doorbell but found none, so he figured his only choice was to knock on the inner door. He reached for the handle of the screen and found it, too, was so icy he thought his skin might stick to it. The hinges creaked, and the closing spring stretched with a piercing screech. Cooper knocked on the heavy navy-blue wood.

On the very first strike, the door swung open, away from him. All of the house's lights suddenly went dark again, exactly like they had a few nights before. A slow glance back showed the lights of his home were still aglow.

"Hello?" Cooper whispered, his hands now feeling clammy. When no one answered, he spoke again, with more force. "Hello! Is anyone home?"

He reached forward, and the door drifted farther, more than it should have from the force of his light touch. He peered through the open doorway.

As his eyes adjusted to the darkness, Cooper found it hard to breathe.

Nothing that met his eye was right. This living room, which he'd glimpsed many times through the large bay window, was supposed to hold two off-white couches atop a teal-and-tan rug, a circular glass coffee table with a decorative lamp, and a framed black-and-white cityscape hanging over the mantel.

Except none of it was there.

The inside of the house was exactly as it had been for years; the way it had been until three months ago.

Dark, debris filled, and abandoned.

13

Cooper blinked, then blinked again. He wondered if he was somehow at the wrong house, as if that were possible. He stepped through the doorway, baffled. The enticing smells of pumpkin and fresh paint vanished completely, replaced by a wave of musty dampness, as if the house was filled with nothing but wet leaves. Cooper's tongue felt gritty with the taste of mold and dust, and with each step he found it harder to think clearly.

The house was supposed to hold a gleaming dining and living room painted the color of heavily creamed coffee. Instead, the walls were adorned with faded flowery wallpaper, many sections of which drooped halfway to the floor where the glue had failed. Instead of a modern dining set, a grimy square table stood crookedly in the room, topped with three stained china plates with matching cups, as if a pleasant afternoon tea had been abruptly interrupted decades ago. An ancient, filthy couch with ornately patterned cushions and carved wooden arms sat in the living room, its stuffing escaping through a large hole that looked like it had been gnawed open by some critter. It was all dimly illuminated by moonlight streaming through the shattered remains of the windows on the opposite wall.

Moonlight also came from the middle of the living-room ceiling, where the wooden floor beams of the second story protruded downward, like something large had crashed through them, allowing light from an upstairs window to filter through.

Cooper pulled his phone from his back pocket and turned on the flashlight. The beam was clouded by the heavy air, thick with foglike dust motes. He put the curve of his elbow over his mouth and coughed. He shook his head and rubbed his eyes to see if clearing his vision would change the images before him.

Then something shot past his ear.

Cooper screamed and swatted the air around his head. He fell, landing hard on his backside, and his phone skittered across the floor, the beam from its flash bouncing and ricocheting around the walls before it landed light side down. His heart drummed impossibly fast in his chest, and he held his hands at the ready in the darkened room. A rustling and flapping mass cut through the air away from him, coming to rest on the back of the gilded couch.

The inky-black creature turned around and peered back at Cooper in the moonlight.

"Stupid bird!" Cooper shouted, the terror of the previous moment still flooding his veins. The feathered beast tilted its head, first to one side, then the other, as if contemplating the impertinence of this intruder. After a soft, dismissive caw, it moved in a way Cooper would have sworn was a shrug and took flight again. It circled the room a few times, dropped a small "gift," as Cooper's mom might say, next to his hand, then disappeared from the house through one of the many open window frames.

Cooper folded in half and plowed his fingers through his hair. The surge of adrenaline, now gone, left him exhausted. He rubbed his face firmly, grit from his now-filthy hands scratching his skin. Mindful of the bird poo, he stood and dusted himself off. A new, particularly tender spot announced itself on his rear, caused by a brick he had landed on.

He stepped further into the room to retrieve his phone near the fireplace. The hearth was flanked by two piles of kindling, though it wasn't the normal sticks and logs found in most homes. It was a collection of broken bits of furniture. Cooper remembered his parents' discussions about this house over the years, and their arguments about what should be done about the neighborhood's homeless seeking dry shelter within it for the night. Every once in a while, there would be a telltale flickering glow through the windows, of men and women using whatever they could find to start a warming fire. But that was before. Before Elena had moved in with her new furniture and welcoming hearth fires.

Now the fireplace was dark.

Cooper had seen and smelled the woodsmoke that had been coming from this fireplace moments ago. He had watched it drift upward into the evening sky. But when he put his hand to the mantel, he found it as cold as the door handle. He touched the front of the stonework, the inner bricks, the metal wood cradle.

All icy.

He had entered the house with the intention of getting some answers. Now he didn't even know what the questions were.

Cooper scooped up his phone and turned to face the room from a new angle. A staircase on the opposite wall led to the second floor, presumably to the bedrooms he'd previously thought held downy, rose-stitched comforters and pillow piles. Was it all some sort of illusion? Gazing at the hole in the ceiling, the answer seemed obvious.

A sound of something moving came through a doorway in the far corner.

"Elena?" Cooper tried to say, but it came out as barely more than a croak. His brain told his legs to move, to investigate, but he had to force his feet forward, leaving a trail in the dust on the floor like two snakes' tracks.

He put his hands on the doorframe and leaned into what used to be a kitchen. No one was there except a family of mice. They all shot into a hole beneath the cabinetry, the doors of which hung open at a variety of uneven angles. A drawer lay upside down on the floor and a pillow hung inexplicably from the cracked porcelain sink. He panned his flashlight around the room and saw a small table and chair in the corner. A swath of navy fabric was slung over the back of the chair.

Everything in this house was caked in dust. But this corner was pristine, and a glimmer of gold twinkled back at him from the fabric.

Elena's jacket.

"Elena?" Cooper said again. The only reply came from the rodents, stirring with frantic commotion.

He walked slowly to the table and stared at the stitching

for the first time up close. Though he wanted to run a finger over the rise and fall of the thick gold thread, fear kept his hands by his sides. A small trash can stood on the far side of the table, and multiple crumpled wads of paper lay within it. They too appeared relatively fresh. Glancing around to again make sure he was alone, Cooper pulled the papers out one by one, noting a thick layer of dust in the bottom of the can. Whoever had put these pages here had done so recently.

Cooper flattened them on the table. Each of the five sheets had a ragged left edge, torn from a notebook. They were written in delicate and careful handwriting, and though he couldn't immediately tell the order of the pages, Cooper found the opening of what he could see was a letter.

Dearest Mother,

It's odd writing to you, knowing you'll likely never read this, but I find comfort in at least pretending. I can no longer let these thoughts exist in my own mind, alone, without relief.

You taught me a love for the written word, how important it is to capture history, to commit events to the page, yes? You once wondered aloud, "If something is forgotten by all, did it ever really happen? Or was it no more than a dream?" It's a good question. . . .

Cooper quickly folded the pages and jammed them into his back pocket, wanting to read more within the safety of his own home.

It was time to get out of here.

He backed away from the table and spun around, exiting the kitchen. As he passed a shattered window in the living room, however, he stopped. There, through shards of glass, was his home, appearing exactly as it should. Everything on this side of the alley, however, was altered. There was no picket fence. The yard was a dirt patch peppered with litter. The new white porch was gray and weathered, sloping at a dangerous angle with multiple missing boards.

Cooper stepped to the door—a door that, from the inside, looked nothing like the navy-blue one he had knocked on—and peered across the threshold into the backyard.

Picket fence.

Green grass.

Sturdy porch.

He took multiple slow sidesteps back to the broken window.

Dirt patch. Garbage.

He repeated his glance through the doorframe. Fence, sod, landscape lights.

Cooper stepped out onto the white porch and looked at the lovely butter-yellow exterior walls. The smell of mildew and decay vanished the instant he crossed the plane of the door. Pumpkin and spice again.

He stepped back. Moldy.

He went back and forth multiple times, marveling at how the scents flipped back and forth, as if they were on a switch, before he ultimately stayed out on the porch. He walked to that same lower window—the broken one he had peered through seconds ago—and looked through it again, this time from the porch side. Before he got there, he could see that the glass was flawless and new; even the stickum from the manufacturer's label was still visible in the corner.

Through the window, he saw heavily-creamed-coffee-colored walls, decorative pillows nestled on an off-white couch, and a coffee table holding a stack of magazines. A ceiling fan turned languidly overhead, where the gaping hole had been moments ago.

And a raging fire glowed in the fireplace.

He put his hand out to touch the glass, to prove with more than his eyes that it was solid. He ran it side to side, then recoiled at a sharp bite. Blood spilled from a clean, straight cut on the tip of his middle finger.

Cooper ran.

He moved as fast as his legs would carry him, down the creaking steps, over the slippery leaves, through the picket-fence gate, and back home.

He slammed the back door of his house before leaning on it, gasping for air, his mind spinning so fast he wondered if it would break free of the confines of his skull.

"Cooper, I swear, if you slam—" His mom rounded the corner, her face set in stony anger, until she saw him. "Oh my—Cooper, are you okay? What happened?" She hurried to him and grabbed his hand. "Jess! Grab me a towel!"

He was dripping blood all over.

"You're as white as a ghost! How long have you been bleeding?"

"I don't . . ."

She led him to the kitchen sink, almost colliding with Jess as she came running with a dish towel. Jess's eyes went wide at the sight of her brother. "Oh my g— Did she hurt you?"

His mom held Cooper's hand under the tap as he hissed at the sting of it, before she wrapped the wound with the towel and guided him to a chair. "Cooper, what happened?"

"I . . . I just . . . I cut it over at Elena's house. It was an accident."

"Elena? Who's Elena?" his mom said, putting pressure on the cut.

"The girl across the alley," Cooper mumbled through a wince.

"What girl?"

"The one who moved in this summer."

"There's a girl over there?" His mom took her attention off his hand and looked through the kitchen window at the house.

Cooper nodded and cried, "Ouch!" as his mom pinched the cut even harder.

His mom sighed in exasperation. "How many times will I have to email the city about that place? It's not safe."

Now it was Jess's turn to freeze. Slowly she asked, "Mom, what do you mean, not safe?"

"It makes me sad. No child should have to live like that," their mother said with a gentle shake of the head.

Time slowed. Cooper and Jess locked eyes.

"Live like what?" Jess stammered.

But Cooper already knew. He knew the cozy couches, decorative rugs, and glowing lights that Jess saw weren't really there. None of it was.

"It's bad enough that adults sleep there," his mother said, "but kids? They need a shelter where there's food, warmth, and the hope for some real help. That place needs to be torn down before more people get hurt." She held Cooper's hand up in hers, offering proof of the danger.

A memory flared in Cooper's mind—that moment when they had arrived home from their trip this summer. He had commented on how amazing that house was. His mother had given him that look. "Okay, Cooper," she had said. He had been sure he'd hurt her feelings by being envious. But now, listening to her, he understood her expression for what it was: she had thought Cooper was being a sarcastic smart aleck.

"Oh no," he whispered.

"I'll call the city tomorrow," his mother went on, still squeezing his hand. "Nothing can be neglected for that long without its falling apart. They could at least board up more of the broken windows and help that girl find a better place to stay."

Jess had turned ashen, and Cooper had a distinct and terrifying feeling of coming unmoored from the ground beneath him.

"Bud, you know better than to go poking around over there, even if you are trying to help someone." She unwrapped the towel to assess the damage. "Who knew being a mom involved so much blood? It's too bad you aren't the one whose blood sugar I have to test!"

Jess and Cooper both stared at their mom.

"Jeez, tough audience," she said with a shake of the head. "That was a joke, you two."

Jess managed a feeble attempt at a laugh. Cooper feared he might scream if he made any sound at all.

"Okay, a Band-Aid should do the trick here. Jess, can

you grab me one from the drawer?"

Jess did as she was told. She moved like she was made of some unbendable material as she crossed to the other side of the kitchen. She stared at Cooper with pleading eyes as she came back to his side. But Cooper had nothing to offer her. The only solace he could find for himself was the knowledge that Jess was as lost as he was.

At least he wasn't in this terrifying free fall alone.

14

Cooper sat on the edge of his bed, motionless, and watched blood seep around the edges of his Band-Aid onto his pajama pants. His bedside clock told him it was 9:30 p.m., but he had no idea how long he'd been sitting there.

Unidentified victims of tragedy, all wearing the same crest. A house that morphed before his eyes. A girl who connected it all. He had been scared as he ran back across his alley, wondering how Elena's picture-perfect home could shift and change as it had. But to hear his mother talk—to see her utter cluelessness about that house—"frightened and confused" had graduated to "terrified and paralyzed."

Who was Elena, if that was even her real name? Why was she here, perched on her swing staring at him and his sister? If he'd been able to move at all, Cooper would have laughed at the fact that Jess had thought they should warn Elena about the symbol she was wearing. That concern had disappeared as quickly as her holographic ceiling fan. Now he wondered if he needed to warn the world about *her*.

Why couldn't his mother see the house? The fence? The green grass? And at the same time, why *could* he and Jess?

That was when his sister came running into his room, her hastily donned pajama bottoms twisting awkwardly around her waist and her sleep shirt on backward. "Cooper," she whispered, "what the heck is going on?"

He shook his head, bringing on a wave of dizziness. "I don't know." Jess was freaked out, and he hadn't even told her what he'd seen *inside* the house.

"I just asked Mom about Elena when she was checking my sugar." Jess shook her head side to side, trembling. "She's never seen *anyone* in that yard, Coop! She had no idea what I was talking about—she says there isn't even a swing over there. She kept asking me what game we were both playing."

Cooper just closed his eyes and felt the world spin around him. For three months, Elena had been a permanent fixture behind their house, swinging and staring. Cooper had even *talked* to her. She was impossible to miss.

Unless.

Unless she was as invisible to their mother as the yellow paint and chimney smoke.

Cooper clutched the side of his bed with his good hand. "Jess, what color is Elena's house?"

"It's yellow!" she said. "It used to be brown, but Elena's family repainted it."

"And they fixed the whole place up, right? New windows, porch, fence? Renovated the inside, rebuilt the roof? Everything?"

"Yes!"

"Jess," Cooper said slowly, "have you ever seen her parents or anyone else over there?"

Jess shook her head.

Cooper stood and paced, his hands on his head. He stared up at the ceiling, as if the answers were printed on it. He had to tell his sister what he'd seen inside. He motioned for her to sit on his bed and said, "There's more."

He told her every detail he could recall: the dirt and grime, the collapsed floors, furniture that vanished and reappeared, the stone-cold fireplace, the changing smells. He explained how he had cut his finger on a piece of glass that wasn't broken, at least not from one side.

Jess listened without saying a word. She grew paler with each seemingly impossible detail. When Cooper was done, he walked over to where his wadded-up pants lay on the floor and fished the letter out of the back pocket. "And I found this." He unfolded the pages and sat beside his sister.

"What's that?"

"It's a letter that was in the trash, next to Elena's jacket. I think it's from her to her mom."

"You stole it?"

Cooper couldn't help it; he laughed. "Jess, I wasn't really thinking about whether I was invading someone's privacy when I was over there in the Twilight Zone."

Jess bobbed her head.

It took a moment to figure out the order of the pages, then Cooper read the letter aloud.

"Dearest Mother,

"It's odd writing to you, knowing you'll likely never read this, but I find comfort in at least pretending. I can no longer let these thoughts exist in my own mind, alone, without relief."

"What does that mean, 'likely never read this'?" Jess interrupted.

"Maybe her mom abandoned her? Or she's dead?"

"Well, if she's dead, there's nothing *likely* about it."

"Can I please just keep reading?"

Jess nodded.

"You taught me a love for the written word, and how important it is to capture history and commit events to the page, yes? You once wondered aloud, "If something is forgotten by all, did it ever really happen? Or was it no more than a dream?" It's a good question.

"I'm starting to wonder if any of this really occurred. I don't understand the how, the why, or the to what end, but these events did happen, no? All of them? I need them to exist, to be real and true, so I can feel like there's a purpose to it all.

"It's clear now that every quest scars me, weakens me."

"Quest—?" Jess started to interrupt again, but Cooper held up a hand and continued.

"This is all coming to an end soon. I can't take much more. So, Mother, I hope that somehow, some way, you, Father, or anyone, will read these pages and know I was here.

"Please. I need someone to know I was here.

"There must be a worldly order to all these events, but

seeing as how time has no straight lines here, I will start with the quest that is foremost in my memory. Spring of 1911, New York City.

"Wait." Cooper stopped. "1911?" He flipped to the last page, to check for a signature, but he found none. "So this must have been written by someone else, like . . . Elena's great-grandma or something."

But Jess shook her head, eyes wide. "Not if Elena's a *ghost*."

"But . . . there's no such thing as ghosts," Cooper began, but there was hardly any conviction in it.

"Cooper, you've walked through a house that changed before your eyes, you've seen a girl who's invisible to Mom, and you're actually going to sit there and tell me there's no such thing as ghosts?"

Up until today, he'd known that to be true. Now? He tried to find some other explanation, but there wasn't one.

"And look at this." Jess grabbed the letter. "This paper isn't even old. It looks like the notebook paper we bought last week at Target."

She was right. Other than the creases from being crumpled up, it was crisp and white, not some yellowed artifact from decades ago.

Jess found the spot in the letter where they'd stopped, and she started reading aloud.

"The miserable rain woke me, as it always does, in the In-Between."

She paused. "The In-Between?"
Cooper rolled his hand in the air for her to keep going.

"Even now I still find it startling to be awakened wet and freezing, with a building looming over me. I moved as fast as I could as the rain fell in impatient sheets, pushing me toward the house. The instant the door latched behind me, the familiar wave of transformation passed from my head to my toes.

"A quick self-inventory showed scuffed black boots and a faded pink plaid dress cinched at the waist. A thin sweater covered my lean and sinewy arms, and my hands were rough. The life I had entered wasn't an easy one. Of course, the gold-stitched Vigilantes *shield shone from over my heart."*

Jess gave her brother a look, daring him to try to explain this. He said nothing.

"With my chin up, I walked through the building and out the front door. I found myself on the front steps of a five-story brownstone overlooking a sidewalk. A seemingly impossible number of people, all wispy and ghostlike, bustled around, and horses clip-clopped past on cobblestones.

"I wandered the city, searching, but at sundown I gave up and returned to the house to rest, and this became my pattern over the next many weeks. After wandering what felt like every neighborhood, bridge, and street for a month, I started to wonder if I'd been delivered to the wrong place.

"Then, finally, on a Saturday afternoon, I found it: a stone-and-glass building rising ten stories, the words *TRIANGLE WAIST COMPANY* and *HARRIS BROS MEN'S CLOTHING* painted on the outside wall.

"I darted between carriages, crossing to the opposite sidewalk, and ducked inside. A man sat perched on a stool in the foyer, his arms crossed. Though his body was still somewhat translucent, he was solid enough to confirm I was in the right place.

"He would be a victim."

The siblings looked grimly at each other, then back to the page.

"I spoke to him in Italian-accented English and told him that I was reporting to work for Mr. Harris. He shook his head in disgust before hoisting himself from the stool and leading me to a doorway on the opposite side of the lobby. He assured me that my tardiness had likely cost me my job.

"How little he knew.

"He opened a wooden door to reveal a cage no bigger than a coat closet and stepped in, almost filling the space. I despise elevators, especially ones that require me to press against rude men, but when I asked after a stairway, he explained that the stairs stayed locked during work hours so people like me didn't rob Mr. Harris blind.

"With a lurch and a high-pitched hum, we rose skyward. I tried to move away from where his damp body pressed against my side, but there was nowhere to go. I counted the floors with each passing doorway and tried to keep my mind on why I was there.

"We came to a stop at a floor marked with a hand-painted 9. The man opened the door and waited impatiently. I forced the words "Thank you" and hopped off into the narrow hallway.

"A mechanical droning filled the air as I walked toward the lone doorway at the end of the hall, finally

*rounding the entry to a massive room. It spanned the
entire length and width of the building and was filled
with row upon row of tables. Countless women and
girls sat, heads down, at hundreds of whirring sewing
machines. Fabric waited in piles in the middle of the
tables, and spools of thread a foot tall spun beside each one
of them, feeding the hungry machines. Each seamstress's
long hair was swept into a bun to keep it from being
pulled into the spinning cogs as surely as the thread itself.*

"*The lone person standing in the room was a man
who marched up and down the rows, one hand on his
hip, the other moving an amber-tipped cigar to and from
his pinched mouth. The air in the room began to crackle,
though no one could hear it but me. I squared my shoulders and tried to stay calm, but I failed.*

"*I hate dying by fire. It's second only to drowning (of
course). It took an eternity for the echo of those unbearable
flames to leave my skin. Thankfully, however, the pain
always fades. Eventually.*"

Jess lowered the final page slowly, horror on her face.

"Hate dying by fire?" Cooper repeated in a shaky voice.
Every hair on his body stood on end, as if an unseen lightning strike had filled the air with an electric charge.

"Second only to drowning?" Jess read again. Cooper

gently took the letter from her, then scanned the pages. It was ominous at best and absolutely terrifying at worst.

When Cooper finally rested the sheets in his lap, Jess whispered, "So Elena's saying she died in this fire in 1911 and is still around to swing on her swing, talk to you, and write this letter. Was she in the train crash in 1928, and Sampoong in 1994 too? 'Every quest scars me.' Maybe it's Elena who's died every time." She gulped. "And it . . . it kinda sounds like she's the *cause*."

"But how could a child make a whole building collapse? And what about the kid they found in the train wreck?"

"What about him?"

"He was a boy."

"So?"

"Elena's a girl, if you haven't noticed."

Jess shook her head. "Cooper! If someone can write a letter *after* their own death, I don't think coming back to life as someone else is out of the question."

Cooper's mind kept trying to find any explanation aside from the impossible. "We don't even know that Elena wrote this."

"Does it matter?" Jess practically yelled.

"I don't know," he offered weakly. He felt like he didn't know anything.

Jess folded her hands gingerly in her lap and inhaled a

long, slow breath before calmly saying, "Cooper, whether this was written by Elena or someone else, whether she is a ghost or not, whether she has died over and over again or I'm totally wrong—we *know* that Elena is the one with that crest on her chest. And that symbol appears in every horrible accident we've found. They are all connected to *her*."

That much was undeniably true.

15

Jess stood up and walked over to Cooper's desk. "We've gotta read more about it."

Cooper's mind spun like a toy released with a rip cord. "About what?"

"The fire," she answered as she grabbed the iPad and returned to the bed. "What was the name of that building again?"

Cooper scanned the letter. "Here it is. The Triangle Waist Company."

Jess typed the name into the search bar and hit enter, resulting in pages upon pages of links. History.com, Wikipedia, and the Smithsonian all had extensive information on the fire, each proclaiming it the deadliest industrial disaster in the history of New York City. Black-and-white photos appeared as well; one showed a huge room filled with nothing but rubble and ash; others showed details both Cooper and Jess had to look away from.

"Skip the images," Cooper said. "Click on that."

It was a *New York Chronicle* article, dated March 26, 1911.

HORRIFIC FACTORY FIRE KILLS OVER 100

A devastating inferno consumed floors eight, nine, and ten of the Triangle Shirtwaist Factory yesterday, killing 146 young men and women. Though lasting only thirty minutes, it is one of the deadliest fires in New York City history.

Owners Isaac Harris and Max Blanck had required their staff of mostly immigrant girls, aged fourteen to twenty-three years, to work this Saturday given a backlog of orders. Many of the victims were the main source of support of their families.

Though the building itself is certified as fireproof, the room, tightly packed with fabric and sewing machines, proved to be a tinderbox. It is not yet known what sparked the blaze.

Last year, the building had been reported to the Buildings Department as unsafe, due to the insufficiency of its exits. No changes, however, had been made as a result. Only one of the building's four elevators was in service at the time of the fire, and the stairways were locked.

Giovanni Marino, the father of one of the victims, had to be removed by police when Mr. Harris arrived on the scene. He hurled insults and profanities at the businessman, threatening physical violence to him and his family.

Beatrice Moretti, the last person known to leave work before the inferno began, reported no knowledge of how the blaze started, stating all was well when she left.

Scores of men and women sought their relatives, but identifying so many individual victims proved impossible. Fifty-six unfortunates will be buried in a group grave.

Cooper let out a long breath while Jess scrolled farther down the article. Again, pictures of the victims were included, and though Cooper had initially turned away, he now knew what they had to do.

"Jess, zoom in."

"Where?"

He pointed at the photos, and when Jess hesitated, he took the iPad himself. He centered one of the pictures of the girls and pinched out, making the image as large as possible.

At first he did not find what he was looking for, but after linking to picture after heartbreaking picture, he found it.

There, on the twisted sweater of a small victim in a plaid dress, was the unmistakable stitching of the bird crest.

Cooper felt like a hot-air balloon whose earthly tethers were snapping one by one, listing wildly to one side. Jess was the only rope keeping him from detaching completely. The crest was no school symbol. Elena's outfit was no normal uniform.

Vigilantes Unum was a mark of death.

"Something awful is going to happen, isn't it?" Jess said, in a whisper so low he could barely make out the words. "Something terrible is coming, here in Chicago, and people are going to die."

What could he say? How could Cooper deny his sister's grim conclusion? They'd found the crest in the rubble of three disasters.

"Coop," Jess said. "I'm scared."

He put an arm around her shoulders. "Me too, Jess. Me too." He pulled her even tighter as she sniffed and her breathing became ragged. Cooper's own eyes burned and welled, but he was *not* going to cry. He had already done that once this week, and that was once too many. "It's okay, Jess. I don't get what's going on, but it's gonna be okay."

He smoothed the back of her hair, feeling the ripples and

bumps of her curls against his palm. It had been a long time since he'd comforted his sister. He used to do it all the time, when Jess's diabetes was new to all of them and she cried with every *pop-click* of her finger sticks. He had been the one to hold her hand and tell her, "It's okay," when she got her insulin shots. They would count down from five and then shout "Ouch!" together, seeing who could yell the loudest to distract her from the pain. But that was before Cooper got sick of the whole routine.

For the first time, it occurred to him that Jess was probably pretty sick of the whole diabetes routine too. But unlike Cooper, she couldn't decide when she did and didn't want to deal with it. She was stuck.

He laughed slightly at the double meaning of "stuck" in his sister's case.

"What's funny?" Jess choked out.

"Nothing," he said quietly.

Jess's breathing calmed over the next few minutes, though not before she left an ample amount of snot on Cooper's pajama shirt. She finally pulled away and wiped her eyes and nose with the back of her hand.

"What I don't understand is Elena's role in all of this," Jess said. "I mean, is she like . . . evil?"

Cooper snorted. "Well, I don't think she's *good*."

"Right. But here's the thing—if these articles tell us

anything, it's that *she's* going to end up dead too. If something bad is coming, she's going to be a victim."

"Can you be a victim if you don't really die, though?"

"What are you guys still doing up?"

Both Cooper and Jess turned toward their mom peeking around the door, her voice tired. "Seriously, guys. I'm glad you've found something to do other than fight, but it's way past Jess's bedtime again, and honey, you know you need your sleep after last night." Her head disappeared, her voice receding down the hallway. "Please, both of you, make better choices."

Jess gave Cooper's hand a squeeze. "I guess we'll pick this back up tomorrow?"

"I guess?" Cooper shrugged. What else was there to do or say tonight?

Jess closed his door on her way out, and the hallway light clicked off. Though Cooper turned his own light off and crawled under the covers, sleep was going to be impossible. Instead, as he lay in the dark, his brain filled with images from within Elena's house. He rolled over, making the bruise on his backside ache. It reminded him of his fall.

Of that bird. That black bird that had scared him. A raven?

Was that the bird on the *Vigilantes* shield?

His mother had been too tired to confiscate the iPad, so

he snuck it under the covers and searched "raven symbols." The results offered absolutely no resassurance. The first article he linked to began:

> *The raven has long been considered a bird of ill omen. As a carrion bird, ravens obtained mythic status as a mediator animal between life and death, associated with dead and lost souls. In Swedish folklore, ravens are the ghosts of murdered people without Christian burials, and in German stories, they are damned souls.*

Cooper clicked off the screen, crept from beneath his blanket, and tiptoed to the window, staring into the night at Elena's house with its soft, friendly glow. Light shone from the two upstairs bedroom windows like eyes. Smoke continued to rise from a fire he knew wasn't burning. Cooper stared until his eyes ached, blinking only when tears started to spill over the edges of his lower lids.

One of the two lights turned off and then on again. It was as if the house had winked at him.

Jess was right. Something bad was coming. But Cooper had come to a conclusion Jess hadn't yet reached. One that he was not ready to share with her.

If only he and Jess could see Elena, they were as marked for disaster as she was.

16

"This is what happens when you guys stay up too late."

Their mom poured herself a third cup of coffee and then sat at the table with Cooper and Jess. She looked at them and shook her head. Cooper and Jess shared a glance, too tired and too scared to do anything more than chew. Even if Cooper had had the energy to try to explain it to his mom, he wouldn't even know where to start.

"Jess, how are you feeling?"

"Fine."

On a normal day, his mother's exclusive interest in Jess's well-being would have bothered Cooper. But today was no normal day. As he picked up his cereal bowl and put it to his lips to finish the sweet, cereal-polluted milk his mom always made him drink, his previous concerns seemed so inconsequential. What was the point of worrying about Jess writing texts to Dad if there was some terrible, looming tragedy? What did it matter if he hung out with Zack or Gus?

Cooper froze.

Gus. He had come down the alley last week.

"Elena, this is Gus."

"I picked up on that."

Gus had waved. He had suggested all three of them play a game together.

He could see Elena too.

Cooper's bowl fell from his lips, bounced off the table, and shattered against the floor. His spoon skittered across the tile and clanged against the bottom of the refrigerator, the din causing Jess to cry out in surprise.

"Cooper!" his mom cried, but he barely heard her.

"Gus!" Cooper said to Jess.

Jess looked at him in confusion. Cooper shook his head. There was no way to explain until they were alone. "Sorry!" he said to his mom, and crossed the kitchen to get the broom and the paper towels. He swept and scrubbed and dumped the mess into the trash while his mind spun with the knowledge that he, Jess, and Gus were in this together. The three of them were on some terrible team they had never asked to join. The question now was *why*? And who else, if anyone, was with them?

He took the stairs two at a time to his room and stuffed his binder and loose homework sheets into his backpack. Jess was at the door when he turned.

"He sees her too," Cooper said, answering her unspoken question.

"The guy that was here last week?"

"Yes! Gus! When I was talking to Elena, he interrupted us."

"He talked to her? You're sure?"

"He specifically asked her if she wanted to hang out with us!"

Jess hurried to her room for her backpack.

"Guys, you don't have to go to the bus stop for another ten minutes," their mom called over her breakfast as the two of them flew down the stairs.

"We know," they said in unison as the front door banged shut behind them.

An icy wind lifted Jess's bangs and took Cooper's breath away. The vast gray sky was broken only by the skeletal lines of the nearly naked tree branches. Blooms on the neighbor's rosebushes that had been limp yesterday were now crispy black, each one lolling downward like its neck had been broken overnight.

Cooper broke into a jog and headed toward Ms. Dref-fel's house.

"I don't understand," Jess said through short breaths, the contents of her backpack jangling with each footfall. "You, me, and Gus can see Elena and the house, but not Mom? Why?"

"I have no idea."

He *did* have an idea. But he wasn't about to tell his sister *Because I think we're doomed.*

"What are you going to say to him?"

"I have no idea."

"What if you tell Gus all of this and he thinks you're crazy?"

"I have no idea!"

Jess stopped and gave her brother a stare. He pulled up too and said, "Look. The good news is that if he can see Elena, at least we have an ally. I don't know why we're in this together, but we are. At the very least, Gus needs to know what we know, and maybe he can help us figure out what is going on."

"And what if he can't?"

"Well, we're certainly not going to know if we don't tell him. Come on."

With Jess begrudgingly satisfied, they took off again. As they jogged on, Cooper told Jess what he had learned about ravens the night before. She found it as worrisome as he had.

They rounded the stop sign and there was Gus, standing alone at his stop at the end of the next block, bracing against the cold. His sweatshirt, which had seemed too hot when school started, now seemed completely inadequate for the autumn weather.

"Hey!" Cooper called out. They came to a stop beside Gus, panting. Cooper's face burned, and he assumed his cheeks were as pink as Jess's in the chapping air. Their quick exhalations rose in foggy clouds.

"Hey." Gus brightened at their greeting. "What are you guys doing down here?"

"Um . . ." Cooper looked at Jess. She shrugged. "Well, I had a question for you. Remember that girl I introduced you to last week?"

"Elena?" Gus said with a nod.

"I knew it! You *do* see her?"

"See her?" Gus leaned to the side and searched the sidewalk behind Cooper and Jess. "Not at the moment."

"No, no, no. Not now! I mean on Thursday. You saw her, right?"

Gus's smile faded slightly, and he tugged on both straps of his backpack. "What do you mean?"

"And you saw her house too, right? The yellow one behind

the swing?" Cooper had to stop himself from grabbing Gus's arms and shaking him.

"Yeah . . ." He stretched the word out like a rubber band.

"So this is going to sound weird, but my mom doesn't see any of that."

Gus didn't say anything. Instead he tipped his head for Cooper to go on, as if waiting for him to add something that would make more sense.

A car pulled up to the curb, and the two young boys who also boarded at this stop piled out. They were already in full-on Arctic explorer mode, bundled in winter coats, gloves, hats, and scarves. They stood beside Cooper and Gus, arms propped out six inches from their sides, like overstuffed teddy bears. Their mother shouted, "Have a great day!" and then sat idling, thumbs moving over the screen of her smartphone, awaiting the bus's arrival.

Cooper grunted with exasperation as the two seventh-grade girls rounded the far corner, their laughter ringing out as if it were any normal day. To his dismay, Gus took a few steps to the side, allowing space for the girls between them. A scent of sewer gas wafted up and around them from a nearby manhole. It seemed a fitting smell for how well this was going.

"He thinks we're nuts," Cooper muttered to Jess.

"Yeah, well . . ."

The two girls stopped talking long enough to give Cooper an unkind glare, assuming he'd been one of the kids making fun of them the other day. *That wasn't me!* he wanted to say. On the other side of him, one of the little brothers punched the other in the arm, and a tussle broke out between them. Cooper, who normally would have intervened, decided to let it play itself out since the two were basically bubble wrapped. Their mother didn't even notice.

It wasn't long before the school bus came to a halt in front of them and the yellow door opened with a clunk. The little boys boarded first, still slapping at each other, followed by the two girls. Gus held a hand out, ushering Jess and Cooper aboard ahead of him, but he said nothing.

Cooper climbed the stairs and proceeded to his usual seat. Instead of allowing Jess to peel off partway down the aisle, he took her hand and pulled her with him. She gave him a firm thank-you squeeze, and they took a seat near the back. He was disappointed but not surprised to see Gus take his normal position up front.

Zack, already seated behind them, said "Hey, guys! Why're you at this stop?"

"Oh, Jess and I had some stuff we needed to talk about." Was it possible Zack could see Elena as well? Was it something kids could do, but not adults? How did you ask someone if they could see something they very well might not be able to see? He couldn't readily say, "A few of us appear to be having a shared hallucination and wondered if you are, too?"

Cooper hooked his elbow over the back of his seat and turned. "Zack, what do you know about the house behind mine?"

"What do you mean?"

"I don't know. It seems kinda weird, right?" It was the best Cooper could come up with.

"Well, yeah. I don't really know anything about it, but I think Tyler and his friends snuck in there a few weeks ago. I could ask him about it, if you want?"

Snuck in.

No one "snuck in" to occupied houses.

Not only did Zack not see the yellow house the way Cooper, Jess, and Gus saw it, apparently neither did Tyler or any of his buddies.

"Jess, are you okay?" Zack asked.

Cooper looked at his sister. She looked slightly green. "I don't know," she finally said. "I don't feel very well."

"I've got a granola bar," Zack said, familiar with her diabetes. He started to dig through his backpack.

"No, Zack. That's okay," she declined.

"Is your sugar low?" Cooper asked, fearing yet another

curveball from this day. "Do you need to go to the nurse when we get to school?"

Jess shook her head, then leaned on Cooper's shoulder. "No. My blood sugar's not the problem."

"Yeah." Cooper nodded. "I hear ya."

They both watched the back of Gus's head all the way to school.

17

Cooper scanned the hallways for Gus all day, to no avail. They had no classes together, but he usually saw Gus at his locker or in passing. He wasn't in the lunchroom, nor was he in Mrs. Wishingrad's old room when Cooper walked by.

When Gus's seat was empty as Cooper boarded the bus at the end of the day, he had to assume Gus had gone home early. He chucked his backpack in frustration onto the seat beside him, only to watch it bounce and tumble to the floor, pouring its contents beneath the bench in front of him.

Zack sat a few rows farther back than normal, joking around with some of their classmates. As Cooper picked up all his papers, he hoped Zack would still have his back if the cool kids made fun of him. But Cooper also knew there was only so long he could expect Zack's loyalty.

Jess made it onto the bus at the last minute and took advantage of the open seat by her brother. "Where's Gus?" she asked.

"I don't know."

"Did you talk to him?"

"No. I never saw him again after this morning."

Jess appeared to find this answer as unsatisfying as Cooper felt saying it.

Cooper, Jess, and Zack climbed off the bus at their stop, and said their goodbyes as Zack headed up his driveway. After he was out of earshot, Jess asked, "Are you and Zack still friends?"

"Yeah," Cooper said with a shrug. "I guess."

"You should invite him over more."

"What?"

"It's just, I mean, I don't think you can really stay friends with someone if you never hang out."

Cooper shook his head. He and Jess had shared more in the last week than they had in the last year, but he still had no interest in talking to his sister about how he managed his friendships. "Thanks for the input," he said, each word sharp.

"I think—"

"Don't."

"It's—"

"Stop! It's none of your business. You wouldn't get it anyway."

Jess's face fell, and Cooper felt the familiar stab of satisfaction in shutting her up. But he also knew she was only trying to help. A tiny part of him wanted to mumble *Sorry*.

Jess turned to go into their house, but Cooper stopped her with a gentle hand on her elbow. "Hey, come with me over to Gus's. I don't want to wait another day to talk to him about Elena, so let's go to his place together and see if he can come over."

She looked like she was trying to decide whether to forgive him for snapping at her. She squinted in the direction of Gus's bus stop. "Do you know which house is his?"

"Yup." Cooper took a step down the sidewalk. "Ms. Dreffel's his grandma."

Jess didn't move. "You know," she said after a moment, "I think maybe it'd be better if we call him."

"I don't have his number." Jess grimaced, and Cooper took a couple steps back to her. "Look," he said. "I don't want to go to Ms. Dreffel's house any more than you do, but there's no other way."

"If he went home sick, he probably can't come over anyway."

"You know what I think? I think you're afraid to go near her house."

"What *I* think is that Ms. Dreffel is going to bake us into a pie."

The joke brought much-needed levity to what had otherwise been a grim last twenty-four hours. Cooper erupted in laughter. Jess started giggling too, amused as much by her brother's reaction as her own joke.

After a moment, Jess nodded. "Fine. I'm in. But it's your fault if she eats us alive."

If the two of them had thought the old woman's house was uninviting from the sidewalk, they found it downright repellent up close. The front steps wobbled with their weight as they climbed them, and the doorbell button was missing from its rusty casing, looking like it might electrocute them if they stuck a finger into the hole. Cracked and flaking paint covered the doorframe, and a handwritten NO SOLICITORS! sign hung crookedly on the door, secured with a thumbtack.

"Are we solicitors?" Jess whispered.

"I don't think so," Cooper said, though he wasn't a hundred percent sure what the word meant.

He knocked.

They stood on the steps, turning their backs to the

wind. When there was no answer, Cooper turned back to knock again but stopped with his fist in the air when he saw a curtain move. He waited, assuming whoever had peeked out at them through the little window would open the door, but nothing happened. He inched closer to the window and tried to peer in, but there were no gaps around the sun-bleached floral fabric that now hung flush against the glass.

"I don't think anyone's home," Jess said.

"But I just saw someone look out this window."

Cooper knocked again and was jolted this time by an immediate, high-pitched screech from behind the door.

"Go away! Can't you read?"

Jess's eyes went wide, and she took a step back.

"Hello? Ms. Dreffel?" Cooper said loudly. "We're here to see Gus."

"I said GO AWAY!" came the reply over his.

"But—"

"LEAVE! OR I WILL CALL THE POLICE!"

A sound like an angry cat followed this, then the sound of something heavy dragging against the floor. Was she moving a piece of furniture against the door? Jess was already run-walking down the steps when Cooper spun and followed. It wasn't until they were around the corner and out of sight of the house that they slowed.

"What the heck?" Jess said.

"Wow. Gus said he likes to get out of the house, but jeez, how could he ever stand to be *in* it?"

"Hey! Guys!"

Jess and Cooper turned to see Gus running to catch up with them. He was pink faced and winded by the time he reached them.

"Hey!" Cooper said. "We were just at your house."

"Yeah." He paused to take a few breaths. "I heard." He laughed and then pantomimed someone ranting and raving.

"Did you go home sick or something? I didn't see you all day."

Gus stood up a little straighter, grinning. Apparently, the weirdness of their conversation at the bus stop that morning hadn't completely driven him away. "I'm all good—I had a note to leave early to help take my grandma to the doctor."

"Did they prescribe anything to make her less of a witch?" Jess said.

Cooper elbowed her. "Jess!"

"What? It's true!" she said.

Gus laughed. "Yeah. She doesn't like people coming to the house."

"We noticed," Jess said. "She sounds hideous."

"JESS!" Cooper said.

"Yup! That's my grandma!" Gus said, still smiling. He bounced a little on his toes as he said, "So, you wanna hang out?"

"Yeah, we do," Cooper said. "Come on."

18

Though Cooper had never hung out with a friend and his little sister at the same time, Gus didn't seem to mind if Jess was around, and Cooper found his attitude contagious. Despite the weight of the conversation Cooper knew they needed to have, they made easy chitchat in the kitchen before Cooper cocked his head for the two of them to follow him upstairs.

On the way to his room, they passed a recent family portrait of Cooper, Jess, and their mom on the table at the top of the stairs.

"Oh! Is this your mom?" Gus said, picking up the frame. "I've seen her biking in the neighborhood."

"Yup."

"Jess, you look exactly like her!"

Jess beamed. There was no bigger compliment for her than being compared to Mom.

"Do you guys want to play Low Budget?" Gus asked. "We have three players again."

Again.

Cooper had been pondering how to talk about Elena after their shaky start that morning, and this seemed as good an opportunity as any. "Gus, can you come over here a sec?" He walked into his room, to his window, and peeked through the curtain.

Elena was there, as she always was, swinging and staring up at him.

"What do you see down there, across the alley?"

Gus joined him. "You mean Elena?"

Cooper took a deep breath, then began. "Okay. So, I wasn't kidding this morning when I said that my mom doesn't see Elena. She's apparently *never* seen her, even though she sits out there all the time. Staring at us."

Gus smiled and said, "Yeah, I had a friend back home who my mom used to call Snuffleupagus because she didn't meet him for two years. Like, he could never come over to play, so she joked around that he was like my imaginary friend."

167

"You're not hearing me."

"He finally came to my birthday party and my mom said—"

"Gus! My mom *literally can't see her*." He jabbed his finger toward the window. "Or her house. Neither can Zack, or his brother. Like, *not at all*. As far as we can tell, the three of us are the only ones who know Elena exists."

Gus turned to Jess as if to check if she was hearing this. She stared blankly back at him from her seat on Cooper's bed and nodded. His expression faltered. "I don't . . . really know what to do with that."

Cooper laughed darkly. "Yeah, neither do we."

"And we found a letter," Jess added. "Elena wrote it, and we think that maybe she's a ghost."

Cooper had thought it better to tell the story gradually, leave the letter for last, but clearly Jess had different ideas.

Gus started to speak multiple times before managing, "What are you even talking about?"

"In the letter," Jess said, "she talks about all these ways she's died."

Gus went still and then spoke in a very slow manner, like he was trying to explain a concept to someone who wasn't very bright. "That's . . . weird. And not actually possible."

"Agreed," Cooper said, nodding vigorously. "But that's

what the letter said. And yesterday, my mom described that house as a place that needed to be boarded up, and today Zack told me his brother snuck into the house recently, like it was still abandoned. Which it was, until a few months ago."

Gus's gaze darted between Cooper and Jess. He looked like one of those cartoon haunted-house paintings where only the eyes move.

Cooper gestured for Gus to take a seat on his bed. "And there's more."

"More?" Gus said, slowly lowering himself to the mattress. "Oh, good."

Cooper recounted the entire story of how Elena's house had changed, and he showed Gus the cut he had received from not-broken glass. Jess crossed her arms and hugged herself as he spoke. When Cooper finished, he sized up his friend, trying to figure out what Gus was thinking, if he was believing anything Cooper was saying. Cooper hadn't even *started* to talk about the raven crest and its trail of fatal catastrophes yet.

Gus laughed again, nervously, then swallowed it down when he saw the serious looks on their faces. "None of that makes any sense. You guys know that, right?"

"Yup," Jess said. "Still true, though."

"Why would we be able to see her, and no one else?"

Cooper pointed for Jess to get the iPad from his bedside table. "That's the crazy part—"

"Oh?" Gus said. "*That's* the crazy part?"

"Do you remember that symbol Elena has on her jacket? The raven?"

Jess stepped forward, tapping. "Which one do you want first?" she asked her brother.

"The train."

One by one, they walked Gus through the three articles, starting in England. With each photograph of the crest on the victims' belongings, a groove between Gus's eyebrows grew deeper and deeper. After the final series of photos from the Sampoong Mall, Gus finally spoke. "How did you guys even find these?"

"The magic of Google," Cooper said.

"So," Gus said, closing his eyes and putting his hand to his forehead, "you're telling me there's an invisible dead girl who lives in a shape-shifting house across your alley, and you think she's connected to three deadly accidents that happened decades ago, all over the world?"

Cooper, expressionless, said, "Yes. That's basically right."

Jess added, "We couldn't find that raven symbol *any-where* online other than in these catastrophes."

"Okay, well," Gus started, a humorous lilt to his voice, "it's not like you're going to find news articles in the paper

170

like 'Local Girl with Raven Symbol on Sweater Buys Groceries,' or 'School with Raven Crest Happy to Report No Catastrophes Today.' Just because there are no articles doesn't mean it's not out there."

Jess crossed her arms and set her jaw.

"I know this is a lot to take in," Cooper said, "but you have to believe us. None of that explains why my mom and Zack can't even see Elena."

"You must have misunderstood them," Gus said.

"What about what I saw inside that house last night? I didn't misunderstand that."

"Maybe it was a dream or something."

"I didn't dream this cut on my hand!" Cooper thrust his finger in front of Gus's face.

Gus flinched away and chewed his inner cheek.

"Look," Cooper said slowly. "You see her too. *You're like us.* I don't know how or why, but we're all part of a weird puzzle, whether we want to be or not. Jess and I think something terrible is coming, some catastrophe, exactly like all of these." He shook the iPad like a lawyer presenting evidence to a jury. "We have to work together to figure it out."

Gus closed his eyes, took a deep breath, and stood up slowly. "You know, I should probably get home."

The letter. Cooper had to show Gus something more concrete. He wasn't proud of stealing it, but he had to convince Gus somehow. It was the only solid evidence he had short of dragging Gus over to the house and throwing him through the doorway, and Cooper wasn't quite ready to do that yet. He went to his dresser to unearth the pages from the bottom of his sock drawer.

"You have to believe us," Jess pleaded softly. "This isn't a game. If you can see Elena, you also might be in danger."

Cooper slumped a bit hearing Jess had reached the same conclusion he had: to see Elena, her house, and her crest was to be in peril.

"You have to help us stop it," she added.

"Stop it?" Gus said. "Stop what, exactly?"

"Whatever's coming," Jess said.

Gus grunted in frustration. "How?"

"Whatever's coming," Jess repeated.

"And that is?" Gus said.

"Whaderz com . . ."

"Jess?" Cooper said. The sound of Jess's voice repeating the phrase snapped him to attention. He spun around, a pair of socks in each hand, and immediately recognized his sister's glassy-eyed stare. She was pale, and a fine film of sweat glinted on her forehead. "Oh no," he said, rushing to his sister's side.

They had gone straight to Gus's house after school—and had skipped snacks.

"Gus, get me some juice!"

Gus blinked at Cooper, bewildered. "What?"

"Some juice! Downstairs, in the fridge." Cooper knelt down in front of Jess and wiped a bit of spittle that was gathering at the corner of her mouth.

"Wherscum . . . ," Jess slurred with grave seriousness, her lips fumbling as she stared at Cooper and through him at the same time.

Gus stood stuck to the carpet, baffled. "What's wrong with her?"

"Forget the juice. Come on, you have to help me get her downstairs. She's diabetic; her blood sugar's too low."

Cooper scooped the crook of his elbow under Jess's armpit and heaved her to her feet. Gus did the same on the other side. The two of them shuffle-stepped beside Jess, helping her to awkwardly cross the room. She mumbled, "Whatever's coming," three more times, each less intelligible than the last, as Cooper and Gus lift-dragged her down the stairs, through the hallway, and into the kitchen. Cooper's heart was pounding. He knew exactly what he needed to do, but that didn't mean he wasn't afraid. Fear had moved in the day Jess was diagnosed and was always lurking around the edges of the house.

"What should I do?" Gus asked, his gaze skittering around the kitchen.

"Help me get her into this chair." Cooper used his foot to drag a seat out from under the kitchen table, and as Jess hit the wood, he bolted to the refrigerator.

"Damn!" He tilted the orange juice container in front of his face; there was maybe a tablespoon left pooling in the corner of the clear plastic. He poured it into a glass anyway, added a mounding scoop of sugar from the bowl next to the coffee maker, and filled the rest of the glass with water. He snatched a dish towel on his way back to the table.

"Jess. Drink." He held the glass to her lips with the towel beneath.

At first it dribbled down her chin and onto the fabric. She spluttered, "Whas . . . ," which opened her lips enough for Cooper to get some of the liquid into her mouth. The taste of it appeared to shock Jess at first, but then, with an eager awareness, she raised her hands, grabbed the glass, and gulped the remainder down.

"What happens now?" Gus asked, watching Jess with wide eyes.

"Give it a sec. I'm going to make her a sandwich."

Over the next few minutes, as Cooper hurriedly spread thick layers of peanut butter and jelly onto bread, Jess became Jess again. She blinked multiple times and looked around with a confused gaze. She soon realized what had happened. "I went low again, huh?"

Cooper set the plate in front of her and filled her glass with milk. "Yup. Eat."

Jess nodded and dug in.

The boys sat down at the table with her, Cooper patiently waiting, Gus looking at her warily, as if she were a bomb about to explode. Through a mouthful of peanut butter, she said, "I'm okay, Gus, chill. Where were we?"

"We were telling Gus about the crest."

"Right." Jess swallowed some milk and brought the glass back down firmly against the table. "You have to help us stop whatever's coming!"

Gus flopped back in his seat, stunned and a bit exhausted by Jess's remarkable recovery from a medical emergency. "I don't even . . . Jess, are you okay?"

She waved his concern away like a fly. "I'm fine. Are you going to help us?"

With a small laugh, Gus said, "Umm, okay, I guess we're back to that. Look, if I believe you guys, and that's a big if, answer me this: how are we supposed to stop some big catastrophe from happening if we don't even know what it is?"

"We have to go talk to Elena. Make her tell us everything she knows," Cooper said.

"And if she doesn't want to tell us anything?"

"Well, then at least we tell her what *we* know," Cooper

said. "And you can help us study those old events, or maybe find more."

"Yeah," Jess added, "I think we should go to the library and search through old newspapers that might not be online. Three of us would get way more done than two."

"Exactly," Cooper said. "Maybe . . . maybe there's a pattern to these disasters. If we can figure it out, we might be able to stop the next one."

"Stop Elena," Jess said ominously.

Gus took a slow breath. While he considered what they were asking, Cooper and Jess went through the ritual of checking her blood sugar. "Five, four, three, two, one, ouch," they both said, mechanically. *Pop-click.* For the first time, Jess didn't flinch when Cooper poked her finger. A needle was the least of her worries.

When all was done, Cooper took his sister's hand, this time for solidarity. "Gus, we need as many brains on this as possible. If we're wrong, we're wrong, and all three of us can laugh later about how stupid and crazy we were. But if we're right . . ."

He fell silent as Gus stood. For a moment, he thought Gus was going to take their hands as well. But then Cooper's heart sank as Gus walked to the back door and grabbed the knob. Jess started to speak, but Cooper squeezed her hand

and gently shook his head. They had said all they could. They had tried.

But then Gus turned back to them, fished his phone out of his pocket, and said with a small, sad smile, "Well, let me call my grandma. I need to let her know I'm going to be gone awhile."

19

Ms. Dreffel apparently didn't like the idea of Gus staying late, or so it seemed as Cooper and Jess watched Gus out by the garage on his phone. He paced the driveway, talking intently, while they stayed in the kitchen to give him some privacy. Elena had apparently decided to do the same, having gone inside when Gus walked out to place his call. It didn't look like it was going well.

"Grandmas, huh?" Cooper said to Jess.

She just nodded, her eyes locked on Gus, her expression blank. "I guess they're all nightmares."

Cooper knew he and Jess were thinking about the exact same thing. It was impossible for anyone to mention grandmothers without both of them being immediately transported back to that day, three summers ago, when they'd seen their own grandma for the last time. Their father had moved out six months earlier, and they were going to their grandmother's house to see him; it was going to be only the second time Jess and Cooper had done so since he'd bailed on them.

Their mother had driven them to the gated entrance to Grandma Stewart's house, but Cooper hadn't budged from his place in the front seat. "Go on," his mother had said. "And be nice. Your dad and your grandmother are family forever, no matter what."

That wasn't the attitude you had when you were yelling at Dad on the phone last night, Cooper thought.

"Let's go," Jess said from the back seat of the car. She hopped out and stood waiting, bouncing slightly as she smiled up at Grandma Stewart's home, beyond the ornate iron fence and the tall hedges.

Jess was still naive enough to be excited about going over to Grandma Stewart's house, with its massive rooms and huge swimming pool. Cooper, however, found this whole "play nice" charade with both his grandmother and his dad tiresome. "Mom, can I just stay with you?"

"I'll be back in two hours."

"Can you at least come in with us?"

Their mother smirked. "Trust me, we are all better off if you guys head up that driveway alone." She gave him a gentle nudge.

She was right. It was no secret that Grandma Stewart thought Cooper's mom was the biggest mistake of his dad's life. Years ago, his parents had happily recounted stories of rankling Grandma Stewart's sensibilities: hanging spoons from their noses at her Thanksgiving table, standing barefoot on a beach to exchange vows, getting busted skinny-dipping in her pool at two a.m. (an act Cooper couldn't imagine his dad doing now). Cooper's grandmother openly bemoaned his mom's lack of polish and refinement, but it was clear to Cooper that this was just code for what his mother really lacked: wealth. She had never been, nor ever could be, good enough for Grandma Stewart's son.

But it had never seemed to matter to Dad . . . until it apparently did. In a moment of quiet reflection after Dad had moved out, Cooper's mom had told him, "Your father and I have a different idea of what it means to 'grow up.'"

Cooper peered at the long driveway leading to his grandmother's grand estate. Though he was nervous about seeing Grandma Stewart—the term "cold fish" would actually be a generous description—he was far more concerned with how to talk to Dad.

"Buddy. You gotta go." His mom prodded Cooper

again with an elbow. "Your dad loves you and wants to see you."

He dragged himself from the car and didn't turn when his mother gave three friendly honks as she drove away. He did smile, however, because he knew the sound irked his grandmother.

One of his grandmother's numerous housekeepers answered the door and led Cooper and Jess to the back of the house, where Grandma Stewart met them poolside, her huge, floppy sun hat shading her tan, leathery face. "Hello, children." Her eyes scanned their clothing and forced a smile. "Do you have your swimsuits?"

"Yup!" Jess said.

Cooper held out his bag as evidence.

"Good. Why don't you go change, and I will have Mary make us some lunch. You're hungry, yes?"

They both nodded.

Cooper never knew quite how to act at his grandmother's home. After all, who wouldn't love a giant pool, endless snacks, and an in-home theater with seats like the ones at the movies? Jess sure did. It was a kid's wonderland. Except that actual kids didn't seem particularly welcome. There were endless shushings and demands to slow down if they moved any faster than a walk. And when Cooper and Jess swam, they had to be careful not to splash too loudly, or

Grandma Stewart would yell at them to stop behaving like wild animals.

"Where's Dad?" Jess asked as Grandma Stewart turned toward the kitchen.

"Your father was called in to the hospital."

Jess sagged. "Really?"

"Jessica, it's not as if your father can plan when some unfortunate soul has a heart attack. You should be thankful that he is there to help them."

Jess stared at her feet.

Cooper, on the other hand, exhaled in relief. He felt a hundred pounds lighter as they walked to the room next to his grandmother's study to change. That weight, however, appeared to have slid off him and landed squarely on top of his sister.

Cooper was out of the changing room fourteen seconds later, and he stood waiting for Jess. He took in the familiar doorway that led to his grandmother's office, a room that was like something out of a BBC miniseries with its leather, dark wood, and meticulous organization. Except this time, there was an out-of-place bright blue envelope lying on the floor halfway to the desk.

Cooper squinted slightly and saw his father's name in the return address corner. He peered around the hallway to see if anyone was coming before stepping into the study.

The envelope was addressed in a calligrapher's curly, fancy script. His father's name wasn't the only one in the upper left corner. It said *Dr. Robert Stewart and Dr. Janice Brown* above his dad's new address.

Cooper bit down hard on his bottom lip as he found himself breathing quickly, heavily. Who was Dr. Janice Brown? The only envelopes he had ever seen like this in the past were for important invitations, like bar mitzvahs and weddings. Was his father getting married again? Surely he wasn't allowed to remarry when the divorce wasn't even official yet.

Cooper picked up the envelope with numb fingers and turned it over. The flap dangled open, and he gripped the thick paper within. It stuck a bit as he tried to slide it out. He ripped the envelope to get it free, not caring that he was leaving evidence that he'd been snooping.

Cooper blinked. Staring up at him from the card was a photo of a baby.

It was swaddled and smiling in a towel with cartoon yellow rubber duckies and bubbles floating around the edges. The words at the bottom read: *Rub a dub dub, there's a new baby in the tub! Robert Mitchell Stewart Jr. is here!*

Cooper understood that his parents' marriage was over. He had started to wrap his head around the idea that he would have to spend time between two different houses, one for Mom and one for Dad. He was even a bit relieved that the arguments and tension in the house had moved out with his dad.

But Dr. Janice Brown?

Robert Stewart Jr.?

"What are you doing?"

Cooper snapped his head up to see his sister at the door. "You need to get out of there!" Jess whispered. "You know Grandma doesn't like us in her office."

Cooper looked back down at the card in his hand. There was more written below the name.

Born June 3. 6 pounds 10 ounces, to proud parents Robert and Janice.

Last month.

"Children?" Grandmother Stewart's voice came from the end of the hallway. Jess's head snapped to the side. She turned back to Cooper with eyes like saucers and backed away from the door to make room for the old lady to swoop into the room.

"What are you doing in my office?" she demanded as she rounded the corner.

He clutched the envelope in one hand, the announcement in the other. Despite standing red-handed before his grandmother, he wasn't nervous or afraid. All he felt was anger. Breaking house rules didn't matter. Being disrespectful didn't matter. Nothing mattered, except what was in his hand.

He held the announcement up like a soccer referee presenting a red card. Foul play! Serious offense!

Grandma Stewart squinted, crossed her arms, and leaned against the doorframe. "You don't mean to tell me your mother hasn't told you about this, do you?"

Cooper's hand began to shake, and he pursed his lips as hard as he could. His throat felt like it was closing. He couldn't breathe.

Behind his grandmother, Jess—still clueless as to what they were talking about—was looking back and forth between the two of them.

"I shouldn't be surprised," his grandmother went on. "Your mother has always preferred to live in some dream world rather than the real one the rest of us live in. Did she honestly think you'd never find out?"

"Find out what?" Jess squeaked.

Cooper couldn't say it. He wouldn't say it. He knew that Jess still thought there was a chance their father would waltz back in the door, plant a kiss on their mom's cheek, and announce he was home to stay.

Grandma Stewart shook her head. "Jess, your father and his soon-to-be-wife have had a baby. You have a wonderful new little brother."

Jess gaped. She looked to Cooper to see if their grandma was joking. "Like, a real baby?"

The old woman sighed. "Of *course* it's a real baby. Honestly." Grandma Stewart walked forward and plucked the announcement from Cooper's hand. "Oh, now see what you've done! You bent it."

Bent, wrinkled, crushed. Ruined.

She looked at the card with a tenderness Cooper couldn't recall ever being aimed at him, then showed it to Jess. "See. This is little Robert Junior."

Cooper didn't realize he had made a muffled groaning sound until his grandmother turned back to him with a disapproving glare. "You know, your father wanted to name *you* Robert Junior, but your mother wouldn't allow it. Not that I was surprised. That family of hers has never had much of a sense of tradition."

"But," Jess sputtered, "Dad only moved out six months ago."

How's that *for a sense of tradition?* Cooper thought. *Betrayal! Pass it on!*

He dropped the envelope and walked out of the office. He went straight out to the pool and fell beneath the surface of the water. Three years later he still felt like he'd never truly reemerged.

"Okay, he's done," Jess said now, scurrying away from

the kitchen window. Cooper took a deep breath as Gus pocketed his phone and returned to the house.

"You ready to go?" Jess asked.

Cooper had to take a moment to remember where they were even going.

"Okay," Gus announced, closing the back door behind him, "I can stay until six."

"Sweet!" Jess said.

They all checked the kitchen clock; it was 5:12. A bit longer would have been better, but they would make do. Jess looked back at Cooper. "You okay?"

"Yeah . . . yeah," Cooper said, shaking his head to clear it. "You guys ready to do this?"

Gus shrugged with a grin. "Dude, I haven't been ready for *anything* that's happened so far today. Why start now?"

They all nodded. They all nodded some more. No one moved.

Gus was the first to laugh, sending Cooper and Jess into nervous giggles. Two deep dimples that Cooper had never seen before appeared in Gus's cheeks. "This is crazy," he said.

"Yup," Cooper agreed. He gave one final huge nod, stepped to the door, and opened it wide.

The yellow house looked as bright and cheerful as ever, but Elena was nowhere to be seen. Cooper and Jess moved down the driveway quickly, but Gus stalled halfway. "So, should we worry about that black cat in our way? 'Cause that sure seems like a bad omen to me."

Sure enough, lying in the middle of the alley like he owned the joint was Panther. His piercing yellow eyes were trained directly on Gus.

"Oh, this is just Panther," Jess said, reaching down to scratch his furry head as she passed him. "He lives next door. He's harmless."

"Uh-huh," Gus said doubtfully. He gave the cat a wide berth as he caught up with Cooper and Jess.

The trio stopped at Elena's gate and stared at the unoccupied backyard.

"I really don't want to go up there," Jess whispered to Cooper. She grabbed his hand and squeezed tightly.

"It'll be okay," he told her. He pushed open the gate and pulled Jess with him. Gus followed as they climbed the porch steps and glanced through the window into the orderly, well-decorated scene within. Sweat collected between his and Jess's palms despite the chill in the air. Cooper was terrified at the prospect of entering the house again, but Jess and Gus needed to see the truth.

"You guys ready?" Cooper opened the screen and held up his fist, anticipating the damp thud of the rotten wood that lay beneath the supernatural facade, but before he could land his first knock, the door swung open.

Elena stood in the doorframe, her usual placid and watchful gaze replaced with a piercing glare, like she'd been taking lessons from Ms. Dreffel.

"What do you want?" she snapped.

Cooper's mouth hung open as he scanned the room through the doorway—a beautiful living and dining room lay behind her. His mouth closed and opened like a fish on a hook as he took in the photo of the cityscape hanging over the mantel and the ceiling fan twirling lazily from the ceiling.

He shook his head and sputtered, "This was . . . but . . . this . . ." He turned to Gus and his sister, pointing an unsteady finger toward the room. "Guys, I swear, this isn't what this house really looks like."

Jess's reaction was unreadable; Gus gave him a shrug.

Cooper dropped his hand, took a deep breath, and said, "Hi, Elena. We were wondering if we could come in and talk."

"Now's not a good time," she said curtly, and started to close the door.

Cooper stuck his foot in the jamb.

"Um, Cooper," Gus began. "I don't think she wants—"

"No, seriously," Cooper said. He wasn't going to let Elena slip away again; they needed to know what was happening. "Now's the *perfect* time. We need to talk."

"No. You need to leave," Elena said, pushing the door harder, painfully pinching Cooper's foot.

"Look! I'm not leaving until you give us some answers. We know that there are people who can't see you, *Elena*, if that's even your real name—"

"Cooper . . ." Gus spoke over him, a fearful caution rising in his voice.

Elena's eyes narrowed more with each new word, and her features sharpened like a bird of prey ready to strike. Cooper's gut twisted with fear, but he continued. "We also know this house is some sort of hologram or mirage, and that terrible tragedies happen wherever that crest shows up." He pointed at the delicately stitched *Vigilantes Unum* crest on her jacket.

Elena swatted his hand away with a loud slap.

Jess put a calming hand on Cooper's shoulder. "Elena," she said softly, "we don't understand what is going on around here, but the three of us are really worried that people may be in danger. *You* may be in danger. We just want to ask you a few questions."

Elena blinked at Jess, her face softening. Jess stood a little taller under Elena's gaze and took a small step forward. "Please," she added, "if you could tell us more about the things you wrote in that letter, it would really help us make sense of it all."

Any blooming warmth on Elena's features iced over instantaneously. "What *letter*?"

"Uh . . ." Jess faltered. She looked to Cooper, her eyes saying *oops*, *sorry*, and *help!* all at once. She then said slowly, "The letter to your mom?"

Elena suddenly reared back and kicked Cooper's foot with such force that it bent his toes back and shifted his foot enough for her to slam the door in his face.

Cooper yelped in both pain and frustration.

"Well," Gus said, turning around and heading down the steps, "this has been a resounding success."

Cooper pounded on the door. "Open up, Elena! You have to talk to us!" But even as he said it, Gus was already halfway across the yard, Jess speeding ahead of him.

"Elena, please!" Cooper knocked a dozen more times. No response. He slowly took a few steps away from the door, staring at it as if he could open the latch with his mind.

"Come on, man! This isn't the way to do this," Gus yelled from across the alley. He was at Cooper's back door; Jess had already gone inside.

Cooper looked up at the yellow house. He sidestepped to the window and peered inside. Elena was nowhere to be seen, but his eyes caught something that gave him pause. The front door, across the living room, stood ajar. That door had been shut a minute ago.

"Cooper, seriously!" Gus shouted. "She's not going to talk to you. Get off her porch before she calls the cops or something."

She won't. Cooper knew. All of this was far beyond the reaches of the law. He returned to the back door and opened the screen. Then he reached out and turned the knob.

It clicked open.

"Dude!" Gus yelled. "What are you doing?"

He pushed the door to Elena's house wide, and without looking back, he walked inside.

20

A bandoned.

When Elena had opened the door, Cooper had wondered if everything he'd seen the last time he was here had all been some dream. Now he was both terrified and giddy to see the dust and decay of the dark and dilapidated interior. It was exactly what he'd said it was.

"Elena!" he called out. The only response was the cooing of two pigeons in the rafters. Cooper took one step to the side to ensure he wasn't in their drop zone.

He moved toward the open front door. With each step closer, what he saw through the opening made him blink in disbelief. There were supposed to be cars and bikes wheeling past on Poplar Street; hydrants, trees, a dog or two on leash. What he saw instead defied understanding or explanation.

He walked to the entry and opened the door wide.

Framed by the doorway, Elena was walking away from him—across a vast open field. Knee-high prairie grass brushed against her legs and closed seamlessly behind her, as if her footfalls hadn't damaged a single blade. Small foothills rose on the horizon where downtown should have been, each banded with stripes of orange and brown; in the distance, only a lone tree stood. The landscape smelled of fresh-cut sweet hay and was lit by a blazing red-orange setting sun low in the cloudless sky.

It could have been Arizona, or Australia, or another planet entirely. All he knew for certain was that they were not in Chicago anymore.

With one hand, Cooper tapped at the air ahead of him as if testing a hot surface, to make sure his skin didn't shrivel or meet some terrible fate on the other side of the threshold. Warm, humid air hugged his fingers, comfortable and welcoming. He looked at his feet, still rooted firmly in the dusty house. He swallowed and took a step forward.

One foot and then the other parted the grass and sank slightly into soft, rich soil. He let go of the doorframe, releasing his last anchor to anything familiar, and took three faltering steps forward into a canvas of amber, rust, and olive. Glancing side to side, he saw that the house was the only structure within a seemingly endless space extending on all sides.

The only other object that looked man-made was a free-standing door, sticking up from the ground twenty yards to his left. It was no average door—it was more like something stolen from a king's castle or a czar's palace, intricately engraved wood embellished with ovals, twists, and whorls covered in gold leaf. The door alone looked like it would cost more than Cooper's entire house.

"Elena!" he called after her; she was now almost a football field away. "Elena, wait!" Cooper started to run after her. The rhythmic swooshing of the grass against his legs was punctuated by the sounds of crickets chirping all around.

He slowed, however, when Elena turned to him with a look of utter terror on her face.

"What are you *doing*?" she yelled. Her voice, incredibly, was as loud as if she were standing right next to him. She rushed toward him, hands outstretched.

Cooper stopped and looked back, scared something dangerous must be approaching from behind—but there was nothing.

There was *nothing*.

The house he had come out of only a few moments

earlier now stood an inch tall in the distance, miles behind him. If anything, the house appeared to be retreating even farther, while the gilded door stood pegged to the exact same spot on his left. Any hopes Cooper had that Jess or Gus had changed their minds and followed him as backup were dashed. Whatever this place was, Cooper was in it alone.

Well, not totally alone.

He turned back toward Elena to find her so impossibly close they almost knocked noses. "Jeez!" he shouted, jumping back.

Elena grabbed him by the shoulders. "You can't be here!" She was shaking and had become even paler than normal; her eyes were wide, lips blanched. She began looking all around, as if searching for something in the wide-open sky.

"Where are we?" Cooper said, the words catching in his pinched throat.

"No, no, no. We have to get you back." Elena grabbed his hand, tugged him toward the house in the distance, and they began to run. Her panic was infectious, and Cooper's pulse raced from far more than physical exertion. He searched the air around him, unsure what Elena was so afraid of.

A raven had appeared overhead—from where, Cooper had no idea, as there were no trees or clouds anywhere nearby—and was keeping perfect pace with them. Cooper cringed and held up his free hand, ready to defend himself against the bird attacking, but the creature soared peacefully, high in the sky above them.

They ran and ran and ran. The house, however, came no closer. The strange door moved no farther away.

Cooper's sense of time stretched out and looped back again, playing hide-and-go-seek with his mind. Minutes turned to hours turned to minutes again. All the while, the setting sun didn't budge. The raven stayed pinned to the same spot overhead in the orange sky, soaring effortlessly without a single flap of its wings.

Elena finally slowed to a walk before stopping completely, shoulders slumped. She pulled her hand out of Cooper's fiercely. "I told her this was a mistake! What have you done?"

"Her? What have *I* done?" Cooper yelled back in disbelief. Panic threatened to consume his sanity as the house shrank even farther away. "I didn't *do* anything. Just make the house come back, and I'm out of here, I swear."

"I can't just make it come back."

"Well then, who can?" Cooper plowed his hands through his hair and turned away from Elena, only to find that a dizzying ledge, one that hadn't existed seconds before, was mere inches from his toes. A raging white-capped river churned hundreds of feet below, extending in both directions. "Whoa!" he yelped, and hurried away from the brink, stumbling and falling hard on his already bruised rear. The sound of the rushing river, imperceptible a moment ago, was now all around him.

Cooper closed his eyes. Maybe this was all an incredibly intense dream. He counted to three, hoping that when he opened them, he might find himself back in his own room, worrying about Jess's blood sugar, or his dad, or Zack. The only thing that changed when he reopened them, however, was that the sun was now directly overhead in a bright blue sky. Paradoxically, the temperature of the air dropped as precipitously as the cliff edge. He squeezed his lips closed and pinched them with his teeth, trapping the scream that threatened to burst out of him.

Elena either didn't notice the seemingly impossible changes around them or didn't care. She charged to where Cooper sat and towered over him menacingly. "How did you get here?"

"How did I get here?" he said, his pitch rising. "All I did was walk through your front door!" Cooper felt like a trapped animal. He desperately wanted to scoot away from her—or stand up and run screaming in the other direction—but the other direction was now a swan dive into a chasm. He stood up on shaky legs and stared her right in the eye. "Elena! *Where are we?*"

"I can't tell you that! You shouldn't be here."

"I agree! But since I am standing in the middle of wherever here is, I think you probably need to fill me in."

They stood, nose to nose, for a long moment, Elena taut as a stalking tiger. The raven, still hanging impossibly in the air above them, cawed distantly. An echo from what he and Jess had read in Elena's letter, however, told Cooper that he might already know where he was.

Elena drew in a slow breath, took a step back, and said in a near whisper, "You're in the In-Between."

21

The In-Between.

Elena had written about this place in her letter. It was, presumably, where she awoke after each of her deaths.

"In-between what, exactly?" Cooper sputtered, his mouth so dry he could barely utter the words.

She pinned him to the spot with a gaze so sharp it stung. "In between life and death."

Cooper let out a small squeak. "Life and . . . ? Am I . . . ?" He held his hands out before his eyes, examining if they appeared different in any way, ghostly or transparent. He didn't remember dying. You'd think that would be a fairly memorable event, but maybe—since he had never died before—this was how it worked? Maybe it *was* as simple as walking through a doorway, out of the living world into this . . . this place.

Elena shook her head. "Cooper. You're not dead."

"Are you sure?"

"Very." She again turned toward the house in the distance, one hand on her hip, the other on her forehead. Then she dropped both hands heavily to her sides and tipped her head up with a low groan. Disappointment and frustration were etched on her features.

Cooper cleared his throat and said, "Well, if I'm not between life and death, then what am I doing here?"

"I'm glad we can agree that that is the *real* question."

Cooper laughed, once, darkly. "No, the *real* question is—*Who are you?* And what is going on? You show up in your crazy house with your freaky raven jacket, apparently invisible to just about everyone, and you live in some alternate dimension between life and death! And don't think I don't know that every time that crest on your jacket has appeared, it's come with a trail of dead bodies."

Elena shook her head, as if she could repel Cooper's words by force of refusal. "You can't know that. You can't know *any* of that! You're going to ruin everything."

"Ruin everything? You mean stand in the way of your plan to kill yourself and hundreds of other people?"

She gaped at him, motionless. "Is *that* what you think?"

Cooper returned her stare, daring her to contradict him, as he began counting off his conclusions on his fingers. "Here's what I think. I think you're a ghost. I think you've died over and over again, and I think you bring tragedy with you wherever you go."

Elena stood stock-still, her eyes still razor-sharp, but her lack of denial told him everything he needed to know.

"So what's the deal?" he continued. "Why do you do all these things? Are you, like, the grim reaper or something? Some sort of death curse?"

Elena wrapped her arms around herself and shook her head. As Cooper waited for an answer, time played tricks on his mind again—hours seemed to pass as he stood there, thinking and waiting for Elena to explain herself. The empty air was suddenly filled with a chorus of caws, startling him and nearly causing him to lose his footing off the ledge.

An oak tree that hadn't existed seconds earlier now stood beside him—half of its gnarled roots protruding above the ground, like it was trying to climb free of the dirt. Three large, beady-eyed ravens perched on a low branch, their heads all tipped quizzically to the left, then, in unison, flipped to the right, their eyes never leaving Cooper.

Elena made a mournful sound and turned her back on Cooper. He took the opportunity to step away from the ledge, only to notice that the cliff edge had vanished as quickly as it had appeared.

When he looked back toward Elena, an antique table and chairs that matched the decor of the freestanding door had materialized, the tall grass tickling the underside of each seat. She was now sitting with her elbows on the table, her head shaking side to side in her hands. She seemed smaller, all her ferocity gone. The whole scene was shaded by a second new oak tree.

Cooper felt a momentary pang of guilt for upsetting her, then balled up his fists. He walked slowly toward the table, testing each step beneath him. For all he knew, another gaping fissure might open beneath his feet and swallow him whole. He tried not to flinch when the still sky-bound raven swooped down and perched on the corner of the table.

As Cooper sat across from Elena, the raven moved her hair gently with its beak, then tilted his shimmering purple-black head back at Cooper, reproachfully.

"Elena," Cooper said hesitantly, lowering his head toward the table to catch her gaze. "Look, if my theories are totally wrong, I need you to tell me the truth. Because, at the moment"—he pointed at the house on the horizon, no bigger than a green Monopoly piece—"it looks like you're stuck with me."

The raven turned from Cooper to Elena, and when she

didn't respond, it pecked the back of her hand. When she still didn't move, it pecked her a second time, harder. Finally, on the third hearty jab, she dropped her hands and looked up. Her face was newly lined with worry. "Okay, okay!"

At that, the bird hopped off the table and, with a flap that fanned Cooper's face, joined the other three ravens on the branch. Cooper could feel their stares like a drill to his forehead. He slowly leaned toward Elena and whispered, "They're listening to us, aren't they?"

Elena looked at the tree, then back to Cooper with a lifted eyebrow. "Cooper. They're *birds*. Don't be silly."

"Oh! Right! Because *that* would be silly." Cooper's voice cracked on the final word.

Elena reached across the table and gripped his hand. Her mouth was set in a grim line, and her eyes were grave. "I am not going to hurt you. I'm not going to hurt anyone. I don't understand how or why you know the things you do, but you've got it all backward and upside down."

"So, if I'm wrong about what you've done at the Triangle Shirtwaist Factory, at the train crash, at the mall in Sampoong, then why are you always there? You have to tell me."

She shook her head. *"I. Can't,"* she said, as if she were etching the words into stone with her voice.

Cooper couldn't tell if she meant she wasn't allowed to tell him or if she was physically unable to do so, but one thing was clear: Elena was desperate. Afraid, even. Her words were a plea. Her touch, her eyes, her voice; they were bare, raw, and earnest. He, Jess, and Gus had it wrong. Elena was not someone to be afraid of. He sat back in his chair and said slowly, "Okay. I believe you."

With this, something in Elena changed. The corners of her mouth lifted almost imperceptibly, the fire in her eyes receded, and her forehead smoothed.

"Is there anything more you can tell me, though?" Cooper said. He looked again at Elena's house in the distance and let out a grim laugh. "We appear to have some time to kill."

Elena turned to her bird friends and then back to Cooper. "Maybe I can tell you how I came to be here."

Cooper nodded, as did the four ravens. Then the birds lifted off as one, cawing three times each. The tree, as if made of sand, blew away by the breeze created by their downy wings, and as soon as they were in the sky, a flurry of light and sound erupted around them.

The field, the table, and the sun were gone in a blink, and Cooper was now seated on a bench at the end of a short pier with a dark ocean expanse stretching out before him. Elena sat beside him, and a gray cloud-glutted sky pressed down upon them. Ships with tall masts, billowy sails, and large crews of sailors bobbed gently in the water. A salty mist coated his lips and cheeks. The ever-present golden door continued to lurk off to their left, standing incongruously upon the water.

"Whoa," Cooper said, surprised that he could still be surprised. "Where are we now?"

Elena spoke above the shouts of men. "We are where it all started."

22

Cooper felt so disoriented, he was sick to his stom-ach. It was like whoever designed this place—the In-Between—had decided they needn't enforce any of the laws of physics. He listened to the voices of the sailors around him; from their accents, he guessed they were somewhere in England, but who knew if clues like that applied here?

"I used to be like you," Elena said. She sat, chin lifted, drawing in the smell of the sea. "I was thirteen years old. I had a family, a home. A life."

Cooper assessed the antiquated suits and dresses of the people walking the wharf. It appeared to be over two hun-dred years in the past.

"Time's funny here," she said, as if speaking directly to his thoughts. "It loops and contracts, but this is a specific time, the moment when it started for me."

Cooper turned and watched a few couples walk past on the docks, the women with their hands nestled in the crooks of men's elbows. "Are any of these people your parents?"

"No. My parents . . . ," Elena said, seemingly lost in thought and staring far off with a sad smile, "were truly remarkable people. They spent their lives exploring the globe, trying to better understand themselves by meeting people the world over. Unfortunately, that is exactly what led to the terrible situation my sister and I found ourselves in."

Elena's expression turned as dark as the water before them, and Cooper waited quietly for her to continue.

"I was twelve when my parents left for South America, a journey my mother had dreamed of for as long as I could remember. The night before they set sail, my mother ordered a grand dinner, all of my sister's and my favorite foods, including pumpkin pie for dessert. But I couldn't eat. Fear filled my belly. I tried to buoy myself with my mother's passion for her trip, but instead I sank with a terrible sense of foreboding. The next morning, my mother stroked our cheeks and kissed us both on the tops of our heads. She assured my sister and me that they'd be home in a few short months. We were left in the care of our governess, Madam

Ghast. She was a hearty Christian woman who believed, as so many said, that children should be seen and not heard. No matter how much my sister and I tried, she seemed resolved in the belief that our childish ways—for we were children, after all—were proof of the devil in us.

"A few months came and went, and then things at the manor began to change. My mother's letters stopped arriving. I longed for her words and her comfort, but everyone else on our estate longed for the payments those envelopes had carried. As I held myself in my room, trying to catch the fading scent of the perfume my mother had sprayed on her previous letters, the workers faded away as well—first the gardener, then the stable hands, then many of the house staff. The details I could recall about my father's face and laugh began to disappear as surely as our dinner portions. After six months, I knew. I didn't need the letter that finally arrived, the one that spoke of yellow fever. I sat on my bed with an empty stomach, crying noiselessly into my pillow, knowing my world had ended."

Cooper's throat tightened. He could relate to the feeling of having lost his family, but he had experienced nothing like this.

"My sister and I became a burden, it seemed. We knew it was only a matter of time before we grew too onerous for Madam Ghast, and sure enough, one evening, she told us to pack our bags to travel the next day to the mainland. She said we were going to stay with relatives, which I knew was a lie because we had none—our parents were only children, and their parents had passed. We woke the next morning and donned our travel coats with the horrible certainty we would never see our home again. We gathered our things by the door early, and before Madam Ghast could join us, I removed a ribbon from my hair and, with quill and ink I had pocketed from the study the night before, I wrote *Beloved Mother* on it and handed it to my sister. She added *Dearest Father.*"

A tender memory softened Elena's features. "She misspelled 'dearest,' I remember, but I didn't correct her. We then raced to the garden my mother had loved so deeply. There was a raging storm pouring down upon us, and the garden had become overgrown and thorny, but we didn't care. Once we were beside my mother's favorite rosebush, I tied the ribbon to a sturdy stem, and we bowed our heads for the only funeral our parents would ever have by those who loved them. Then, hand in hand, we left to face our fate with Madam Ghast."

There were now dark circles under Elena's eyes that hadn't been there before. "Where did she take you?" Cooper asked.

"After she bellowed at us for our saturated state and re-iterated that we were hopeless, she packed us in a carriage to travel here, to this pier." Elena looked to her left and pointed, as if watching a scene play out before her. "Right there, we watched as Madam Ghast handed a small purse to a gruff and burly man. With a satisfied nod, she told us, 'Go on then. You're with him now.'"

"And where was he taking you?" Cooper asked.

"I never found out. Our ship departed an hour later, straight into the jaws of that storm." Elena moved her extended finger to the horizon. As if on cue, a massive cloud formed, alive with lightning. "We sank right out there. Just far enough away to be unsalvageable. Madam Ghast had long since left the pier, and no one else knew my sister and I were aboard. We weren't missed by one living soul. We simply vanished, forgotten by the world and everyone in it. And that is how we landed here, in the In-Between. No place on Earth and no place in the Beyond." Elena stared intently at the gilded door.

Cooper followed her gaze. "Is that where that door leads? Beyond?"

She nodded slowly. "Sometimes I can hear them—my parents—on the other side, but they don't seem to be able to hear me."

211

"What do they say?"

"I can never make out the words, but there's laughter, sometimes, and warmth. Like they are having a grand afternoon tea. Nevertheless, it is locked, and sits there, all the time, taunting us. I can only get away from it when I reenter the living world. And every time I return here, I try the knob, hoping we might have finally earned our way through, but . . ." She trailed off.

"What happened to your sister?"

"Oh, she's in the In-Between too."

"Where?" Cooper glanced around the busy pier.

"She's . . . out in the living world right now. On a quest, like me."

"A *quest*. You talked about that in your letter. What does that mean, exactly?"

Elena released a long breath accompanied by a small head shake. Cooper had apparently asked too much again. He decided to try it from another angle. "How many of you are here? In the In-Between?"

"Just the two of us."

"But what about all these people?" He pointed at a clutch of passing sailors.

"Oh, they're simply echoes of my memory," Elena said, and then, to prove her point, she waved a hand dismissively at the closest man, who immediately became nothing more than a man-shaped mass of dry and brittle leaves that collapsed and blew away.

"But in the Charfield train accident"—Cooper pointed to Elena's crest—"the unidentified child wearing that was a boy."

The pier vanished as quickly as it had appeared, flickering in the same manner as Elena's house had a few days prior. *A few days.* Was that all it was? To Cooper, it seemed like years ago. When everything around him came into focus again, he was back in the grassy field, back at the table. The ominous storm cloud remained as the sole souvenir of their visit to the pier, still lurking on the horizon. It had deepened almost to black and was on the move toward them. The table now supported two steaming cups of fresh tea on saucers painted with dainty vines and pink flowers. Elena was gone. Across from Cooper now sat a young boy in a crisp uniform and paperboy hat.

Cooper startled and gripped the table's edge with both hands. Was this another "echo" from Elena's memory? "Umm, hi?" Cooper said.

With another flicker, the boy morphed. Where he had been, Elena now sat, reaching for her cup.

"Wha—?"

"I can appear to you however I want, Cooper. However I need. Like the yellow house." She sipped her tea.

"Do that again!"

Elena seemed amused by Cooper's fascination. She did as she was asked, this time flickering into an image that caused Cooper to slap a hand to his open mouth. "How about this?" the new person asked. The voice, the grin, and the clothes—it was like Cooper was peering into a mirror, but with an image that moved independently of him.

"Stop it!" Cooper said. "That's not funny. Change back!"

Her laughter continued through her transformation back to Elena. "I've never been able to show this off to anyone living before."

"Please don't ever do that again," Cooper finally managed to say.

"You asked," she said with a shrug.

"It's beyond freaky."

"I suppose it is. I haven't thought about it in a long time. Sometimes even I forget who I was—who I am. I'm here, and yet not. Invisible. Like a forgotten dream."

Elena sipped her tea again and said, "Anyway, the living are so obsessed with bodies. All of this"—she gestured to herself—"it's just a container, I know now. The true me— my core—is always the same."

Cooper stared at her, dumbfounded. He didn't think body switching was as mundane as Elena was making it sound. He had no idea if the girl he saw now was Elena's "real" self, but she was at least in the image he'd become accustomed to. That would have to do.

"Does it hurt to die?" Cooper blurted out the question without thinking and was immediately embarrassed. It was such a strange and deeply personal question, but when she didn't seem bothered by it, he added, "I mean, 'cause you're not . . . normal, right? You're not really a person, are you?"

Elena flinched.

"I mean, you were a person, but you aren't . . . you . . ." Cooper decided to stop talking.

"Yes. It hurts. I can change how I appear, but I'm still flesh and blood, like you." Elena put her hand on top of Cooper's. It was warm.

As they spoke, the clouds had moved impossibly fast, now covering half of the sky. Lightning danced within them.

"So what happens to you? I mean, when you die, you don't really die, right? You can't have, because you're still here. But your body—bodies?—are always found in the ruins."

"I die the same way everyone else does—the body ends. It's left behind as evidence of who was once there, but the soul, or whatever you choose to call it, goes on. I believe most people go on to the Beyond, but my sister and I, well . . . we end up here, every time. I wake up as my original self, until

215

I'm called back out again. A new quest, a new body."

A truth of what Elena was describing dawned on Cooper. "Wait. You've done this more than three times, haven't you?"

"Three times?" Elena asked, her voice lifting.

"Yeah. That's how many accidents we found."

"Oh, there've been many, many more. Unfortunately, not every tragedy is deemed worthy of news coverage."

Cooper thought of the vast numbers of deaths they had already tallied. The idea that this was only a fraction was chilling. "So—what? That's it? You're going to do this for all of eternity?"

"I used to think so, but not anymore. Every time I return, I'm a little more . . . broken. Weakened. Like less of me returns each time. It's hard to explain."

The temperature around them was tumbling, and Cooper was made colder still by a few drops of rain that began to fall.

Elena looked up, seeming to notice the storm cloud for the first time. She spoke quickly. "Cooper, there is only so much a body and soul can take. The injuries of each of my deaths echo in my bones, and the heartbreak scars my mind. They leave both my sister and me ruined, like the body we've left behind, and it takes longer and longer for us to become well again. Soon, I know, I will be too shattered to ever come back again. Neither my sister nor I can bear much more." As she spoke, rain began falling in earnest, splatting into their cups, splashing up in little tea eruptions.

"Surely *then* you'll be allowed into the Beyond, right?" Cooper said.

The sky lit up for a fraction of a second, and then thunder shook the table. Cooper startled, but Elena didn't react at all. Instead she tipped her head and looked at Cooper through heavy lids. Fat raindrops plastered strands of Elena's hair to her face. "I've come to accept that I'll always be in the In-Between, dead or alive. I only wish I knew whether to fear or to hope that this is possibly my last quest."

Cooper had come here with the sole purpose of saving his own life, and those of his sister and his friend. But, as Jess had suspected, they weren't the only ones in danger. "Elena, I know that you said you can't, but you *have* to tell me more. There has to be some way to stop this awful cycle, for you, for me, for everyone involved. Why not just stop doing these quests entirely? Don't leave this place, don't die again. Then maybe you can stay here until you figure out how to get through that door."

"It doesn't work that way," she said. "We can't stop."

"Can't or won't?" he asked.

At that, a lightning strike splintered the oak tree beside their table with a terrifying and deafening crash. The rain began pouring down so heavily, he could barely see Elena through it.

The In-Between was not happy.

As Cooper shielded his head with his arms, he could barely hear himself say, "Tell me what's coming! I don't want you to have to suffer!"

Elena opened her mouth, but whatever she said was overtaken by a rumbling that went from a murmur to a cacophony in a few short seconds, like an unseen train barreling straight toward them. Cooper slapped his hands over his ears and instinctively ducked down, his eyes closed. The roar shook his chest like the skin of a drum and lasted far too long to be thunder. When it came to an abrupt halt, Cooper dared to crack his lids, and found the yellow house standing only ten yards away. A path of freshly torn, muddy earth trailed out from it, and the door sat slightly ajar.

He caught the scent of pumpkin pie and woodsmoke.

"Cooper, you need to leave," Elena bellowed against the driving storm. She pushed Cooper to his feet. "I'm glad that you came here. But I can't risk telling you any more than I already have."

"You have to!" Cooper's mind flashed back to his dictionary search on "vigilante." *A self-appointed doer of justice.* What justice was being served by her dying in these horrific accidents? And what disaster was on the horizon? "Please tell me what's going to happen—I'm afraid all our lives are in danger!"

"You aren't safe here!"

A thousand more questions rushed to Cooper's lips, but another blast of lightning struck the table, blowing Elena back with a cry. The door of the house beckoned.

"Go!" Elena begged.

The earth began trembling under Cooper's feet, threatening to knock him to his knees. "But—"

"Cooper, now!"

His clothes were leaden with rain, and when he took what should have been the handful of steps to reach the threshold, he found it as effective as walking the wrong direction on a moving walkway. The front door, and only the front door, began retreating, as if it were the basket of a slingshot being pulled away by some giant unseen hand.

Cooper ran, but the faster he sprinted, the farther it seemed to stretch away from him. Then, in a terrifying reversal, the door rushed toward him. Cooper slowed and let out a yelp before the doorway swallowed him up, passing over him like a strong wind. If he traversed the inside of Elena's house, he didn't see it, for the next thing he knew, he was on his hands and knees staring up at his own house, sitting calmly across the alley from where he was on Elena's back porch.

The quiet, cool evening air was disturbed only by Cooper's heaving breath and the sound of a city bus stopping somewhere nearby. His clothes were completely dry.

The familiar sight of Mr. Evans's cat, Panther, prowling for mice anchored Cooper back in reality. The kitty seemed wholly undisturbed by Cooper's sudden appearance. It was only when Cooper bolted through the yard, across the alley, and into his house that Panther skittered away with a glance that said, *How rude!*

23

Cooper made it to his own home almost as quickly as he'd shot through Elena's house. He flew through the back door and used the opposite wall to stop himself. He spun around and leaned his back against it, pressing his hands flat against the surface to convince himself of its permanence.

His chest heaved both from the run and from the absolutely terrifying absurdity of all he had witnessed. How would he even begin to recount all of this to Gus and Jess?

To his surprise, the two of them were standing in the kitchen, both smiling at him. Gus folded his arms smugly and said, "She threatened to call the cops on you, didn't she?"

"How long have I been gone?" Cooper panted.

Jess and Gus glanced at each other slowly, then back at Cooper.

"What do you mean, *gone*?" Jess said.

"I was—" Cooper cut himself short. The kitchen clock, the one he had last seen what seemed like a century ago, showed 5:22.

"What day is it?"

Both Gus and Jess said in concerned unison, "Monday."

Only ten minutes had passed since he had left this same kitchen.

"You guys," Cooper murmured, shaking his head. "I was . . . I've been gone for . . ." He walked to his sister, put a hand on each of her shoulders, and held on tightly. "You have to believe me. Elena's house is . . . it's like a portal or something. I went *through* it, and on the other side was this field and then her house was swept away, and I was stuck there for days, years—"

"Cooper," Jess said over him "we were just over there with you."

"—and Elena and I talked for a long time. She's, like, two hundred years old, but she's never died, not really. She said she was between life and death, and—" Cooper only

222

stopped talking because Gus entered his field of vision, creeping up slowly behind Jess, fear and shock etched on his face.

"What did Elena tell you?" Gus asked.

Cooper was immensely relieved that Gus, at least, seemed to believe him.

"She said that the place where we were is between life and death," Cooper repeated. "I told her all we knew about the crest, and she told me that . . . wait, hold on, I gotta sit down."

They all sat at the kitchen table, foreheads nearly touching as Cooper told them everything he could remember about the In-Between: the landscape, Elena's past, the time warping, Elena morphing and her dying in all of the past tragedies. He told them what he now believed: that she wasn't the cause of these disasters but instead played some role he didn't understand.

When he was done, Jess's eyes were wide, and Gus appeared to be overheating, his face flushed.

"Well, if Elena isn't the one behind all of this," Jess said, "what is she? Why does all this terrible stuff follow her wherever she goes?"

"I don't know. But someone, or something, keeps making her do this. She said she couldn't risk stopping or telling me any more. It felt like *she* was trapped. A victim."

"I know the feeling," Jess said with a grimace.

"And," Cooper continued, "she said that she's been involved in tons more accidents than just the three we've found. And every one of her deaths is chipping away at her—that her body and soul can't take much more. Soon she and her sister will be so completely damaged they'll never be okay again. She also insisted that even though we're right about her and the *Vigilantes* shield reappearing, that we're looking at it wrong."

Gus leaned back and slowly folded his arms, staring up at the ceiling, deep in thought.

"We have to figure out why she's here," Cooper said. "It felt like . . . I don't know, like she was trying to protect me from something, staying silent. The big question now is how do we look at it *right*?"

Jess appeared eager to offer an answer, but nothing came. She ended up shaking her head and shrugging. Cooper made a T with his hands like a football coach and ran up to his room. He returned with the iPad, sat back down, and started typing.

"Everything we know is from these articles, right? The answer must be in here somewhere." He pulled up their most recent search, the *New York Chronicle* article about the Triangle Shirtwaist fire. He read it aloud. Jess and Gus both listened intently. After the last word, they all sat, thinking, reconsidering the information. Cooper strained his brain, hoping for a lightning strike of understanding.

"Read another one," Gus finally said.

Cooper went to their search history and clicked on the Sampoong Mall article, reading that one aloud too. Then the Charfield train accident. He had read them all so many times he probably could have recited them from memory, but he wanted to make sure he didn't miss a single word.

After the final sentence, Cooper closed his eyes. Images from the articles as well as Elena's earnest plea to believe her flickered through his mind, but no answers revealed themselves. He opened his eyes again and turned to Gus. "You got anything?"

"Nada," Gus said.

"Maybe we need to find more articles," Jess said. "More accidents."

"We've already been searching nonstop. I don't know how to find them."

"But she told you there were more. If they happened, there would be records somewhere. We just have to figure out the right way to search."

"Wait," Cooper said, an idea blooming in his mind. He started nodding vigorously at Jess and Gus. *If they happened!*

They stared back blankly. "I don't get it," Jess said.

"Elena's exact words to me were that our assumptions were backward and upside down," Cooper said. "We've been focusing on all those people who died, right? Well, what's the upside down and backward of that? What about people who *didn't* die?"

Cooper looked at Jess and Gus expectantly, but all he got were squints.

"You're not making any sense." Jess was starting to sound annoyed.

"Okay. I said she was in more accidents than the three we've found, right?"

"Yeah."

"But that's not actually what she told me. She said she's been on countless more *quests* than we've found. Maybe they aren't the same thing. Maybe there aren't more articles to find because her whole job is to *stop* these catastrophes! To keep them from happening at all."

Gus started nodding, mirroring Cooper and his enthusiasm. "That could make sense."

"What if the incidents we've found were only when she's failed?" Cooper went on. "We aren't finding articles about her other missions because she *succeeded* in keeping those accidents from happening!"

"That would explain why Elena was so upset when you accused her of killing people," Gus said.

"That would make me mad too," Jess agreed. She then added, "Hold on a sec," and went upstairs. A moment later, she returned to the kitchen with the letter Cooper had found during his first visit to the yellow house.

"The lone person standing in the room," she read aloud, "was a man who marched up and down the rows, one hand on his hip, the other moving a cigar to and from his pinched mouth. The air in the room began to crackle, though no one could hear it but me. I squared my shoulders and tried to stay calm"—Jess slowly lowered the letter and stared pointedly at her brother as she spoke the final words—*"but failed."*

"That's gotta be it, right?" Cooper's grin was wide and infectious. "She's here to stop something terrible from happening."

"So maybe we aren't all going to die?" Jess offered with a laugh and a nervous smile. Gus and Cooper joined in the giggles, their anxieties bursting from them like water through a breeched dam.

But the relief didn't last long.

"But she still might fail, right?" Jess continued. "She *has* failed. Sometimes a lot of people still die. The people . . . who can see her."

"I wasn't going to mention that," Gus said, rubbing the back of his neck.

"Even more of a reason to make sure she succeeds," Cooper said.

"But how?" Jess said.

"I don't know yet," Cooper said, "but we have to. And not just for us, but for Elena too. Who knows how many more times she can do this? Maybe we can save ourselves and her at the same time."

"Yeah, her, us, and a couple hundred other people," Gus added.

"Gus!" Cooper said, so loudly that both Gus and Jess jumped. "Maybe that's it!"

"What's it?" Jess said.

"Every one of these accidents happened to a large gathering of people, right? A bunch of people on a train, a group of women at work, hundreds of people shopping in one mall. They were all *together* in one place. Maybe we can help fend off whatever's going to happen if we just make sure we're not all *in* one place at the same time. We can't all be involved in something if we're not there, right?"

"Not where?" Gus asked.

"*Anywhere*. At least not anywhere together. If this thing is fated to happen to all of us, how can it happen if we stay apart?"

"I guess that makes sense," Gus said.

"But what if it's a really big disaster?" Jess said. "Maybe it involves all of Chicago."

"But we know that's not it, right? Otherwise Mom and Zack and Tyler and all of his friends would be able to see her."

Suddenly it felt like there was a ticking bomb someplace near them. Cooper looked around, seeing potential catastrophe everywhere. Was the stove leaking gas? Was carbon monoxide seeping from the heater? Could a refrigerator kill you?

"But we live together, Cooper," Jess said. "And all three of us go to school together. It'll be impossible to stay apart all the time."

"I could pretend to come down with something terrible that keeps me home for the next month or so," Cooper suggested.

"You aren't that good an actor," Jess said.

"Well, you're sick all the time, maybe you can do it."

"I can't fake high blood sugar. It's kind of out of my control."

"You don't have to fake it. Just hide candy in your room and do all the food cheating you've ever wanted."

"Cooper! I don't actually enjoy going to the hospital. I'd rather not die while trying to save our lives."

"Guys," Gus cut in. "Your mom's not going to believe you're sick for a month, and if you skip school, she's going to find out. But it's not like my grandma really cares if the school tries to call home. I can fake sick for a week, and then just skip, at least for a while."

As Gus spoke, this brilliant plan didn't seem so smart to Cooper anymore. In fact, it sounded awful. He hadn't intended to cut his new friend out of his life. A flurry of new questions popped into his mind, fueling his urge to back-pedal on his own proposal. How long would they have to stay apart? How would they even know when the danger had passed? Did they have the power to change the future, or was that entirely Elena's job? Maybe changing their behavior would inadvertently make things harder for her.

"So that's the plan, I guess," Jess said. "Stay apart to stay alive."

"Actually, let's keep thinking," Cooper said. "Maybe we can come up with something else."

"Maybe," Gus said, "but until we do, I should probably go." He stood and took a few steps away from the table. "I'll even leave the neighborhood when the bus comes near the house, in case it's, like, a bus explosion or something."

The dreadful possibilities seemed endless.

"Hey, Cooper," Gus said. "Do you want to give me your number? It's safe to text, right?"

"I'd think so," he said quietly. It felt like very small comfort. Cooper handed Gus his phone to type in his contact information, and Gus sent himself a text so he'd have Cooper's number. As he did, Cooper stared at his own hands, trying to push away the sting behind his eyes.

Gus gently put Cooper's phone on the tabletop and, with a nod, went to the door. He stopped with his hand on the knob. "I'd say see you later, but I guess that's not really true." He gave them a weak smile and a wave before he opened the door and walked out.

24

True to his word, Gus was absent from school for the next two weeks. He texted with Cooper all the time—the latest hilarious horror stories about his grandma, his creative mock-illness symptoms, funny video clips and memes—and the two of them met up a few times at a local park without Jess. Still, there was a cloud of paranoia over everything.

Cooper hated it.

He racked his brain to find a new, better plan, but he came up empty.

Trying to be as careful as possible, Jess and Cooper stayed as isolated from each other as two people could while living in the same house. They were, after all, only guessing that Gus's absence was enough to keep them all safe. Accordingly, Cooper stayed home while Jess went trick-or-treating with friends (giving them and Cooper most of her candy), and Jess stayed in her room when their mother was gone, a feat Cooper knew took every ounce of his sister's restraint. It was the scariest Halloween of their lives.

Any thoughts Cooper had of questioning Elena further were squashed by the fact that the swing sat empty, day after day. He contemplated going back into the In-Between to find her, to let her know what they were doing, but without a guaranteed escape route, the risk was too great. Instead Cooper sat in his room after school, day after day, looking across the alley, wondering if they were helping her at all, or if all of this precaution was for nothing.

Each morning, he rose early and walked to school alone. He ate lunch in his empty science classroom. He walked home solo. *Stay apart to stay alive.* But for the first time in two years, he found he didn't want to be alone. He missed Gus. He missed sharing his weird comic books, his journaling, his Snickers bars. And he missed Jess.

Who knew that was possible?

"When did you start taking an interest in the news?" their mother asked at the breakfast table one morning, as he reached for the front page.

"It's research for school," Cooper lied, scanning every headline, looking for anything that might be a hint at the impending danger. The university had hired a new basketball coach, there was a new tax coming for much-needed roadwork in the city, some CEO was going to jail. Nothing stood out. No catastrophes either.

So far, at least, their plan seemed to be working.

Their mother was home every Tuesday after work, and her protective presence allowed Cooper and Jess to abandon their precautions. Jess had taken to doing her Tuesday homework on Cooper's bedroom floor while he worked at his desk, an arrangement they found as comforting as their mother found baffling.

On the third Tuesday after hatching their plan, Cooper finished his math and walked over to the window. He looked out at Elena's house and asked hopefully, "Do you think maybe it's over?"

"What do you mean?"

"Whatever it was Elena was here for. Maybe our plan has already worked, and Elena succeeded. The danger has passed. I haven't seen her over there once since I went into the In-Between."

Jess shook her head. "What color is the house?"

"Yellow," Cooper answered flatly, seeing her point.

"Yeah, it's not over." As if to prove Jess's point, a small

sliver of smoke rose from the chimney as she spoke. "Until that house is in shambles again, we're still in danger."

They had to stay the course.

Cooper's phone vibrated in his back pocket. It was a text from Gus.

My grandma fell asleep in her chair and her snoring is so loud that the neighbor's dogs started barking.

Cooper snorted and read the text to Jess. His phone vibrated again.

OMG. SO. LOUD.

So that's what that noise is! Cooper replied, followed by a cry laugh emoji.

Seriously. It's like she's choking on a rhino

Maybe u should wake her up

That's the dumbest thing you've ever said, Gus sent.

We're trying to stay alive, remember???

Cooper laughed out loud.

Riiiiiiight

Gus stopped typing after that. Cooper tried to come up with something else to text about but couldn't think of anything. All he really wanted to do was go hang out with Gus—play a game, read some comics, mindlessly watch some YouTube, whatever.

"Jess, would you be okay if I go over to Gus's for a bit?"

Jess looked back at her worksheet, the shared amusement

of Gus's texts sliding off her face. "I . . . I guess."

"Mom's here, so you won't be alone." When she still frowned, he added, "I'd take you if I could," and he was no longer surprised to realize this was completely true. "I just want to hang with him for a bit. I think he's lonelier than we are."

Jess still didn't look up.

"And you can hang out in here while I'm gone." Cooper never allowed her in his room without him. He nudged her in the ribs with the side of his foot. "You know, if you promise not to touch anything."

Jess smiled begrudgingly. "Why would I want to touch your gross stuff anyway?"

"I'll be back in an hour." He looked at his phone and showed it to her. "By five thirty. Promise."

Jess agreed with a nod. "Fine. Say hi to Gus for me. Now get out of here so I can start touching everything."

Cooper laughed and rumpled her hair, which she pretended to be irritated by.

He took the front steps two by two and arrived on Ms. Dreffel's block a few minutes later. Gus was sitting on the front steps, scribbling in his journal, next to a pile of worn-looking comic books.

"Hey!" Cooper called out.

"Coop?" When Gus saw Jess wasn't with him, he relaxed

and smiled at Cooper, but it didn't brighten his face the way it usually did.

"Is everything all right?" Cooper asked.

"Yeah. I just had to get out of there for a bit." Gus closed his notebook and offered Cooper a newish-looking Hulk. "Want to read?"

Cooper took it and sat beside Gus. "Your grandma's not going to scream at me, is she?"

Gus took a comic for himself. "No, she's still konked out in there." He said it with a laugh, but something was wrong. He didn't open his Squirrel Girl but instead stared out at the street, a sick look on his face.

"Seriously, man, what's up?"

Gus rolled up his comic like a newspaper, wringing it in his hands. "I don't know. It's my parents, that's all."

Cooper took a breath. "Did something happen?" He braced himself to hear Gus tell him they were getting divorced. Cooper would've done anything to spare Gus from speaking those words, but he also knew he was as powerless to control what two strangers in Oklahoma did as he'd been with the two adults who had slept in the room next to his.

"Nah," Gus said, "nothing's happened, not that I know of, at least. It's just . . . I've been thinking about them a lot. About how they were always gone, always busy with something else, even when things started to fall apart. I wish that they . . . I don't know, maybe they just don't care about me that much. I haven't heard from them." His voice cracked on the word "them," as if it had shattered in his mouth. "It's like I don't even exist. Like I'm . . . invisible." He gave Cooper a small, sad smile. "Just like Elena, I guess."

Cooper stared at his hands. As Gus spoke, he realized that, whether Gus's parents got divorced or not, the damage had been done. Cooper thought back to that night at the movie theater, that feeling of being completely forgotten by his dad. That was before his parents had split up. The pain started so much earlier.

"I am so, so sorry," Cooper said. He wanted to say something that would erase the feelings he knew his friend was experiencing. He wanted to let him know that one person knew what he was going through and *did* care. But how do you say the right thing when you have no idea what that is? If he'd known the words that healed this pain, he would have tried them on himself long ago.

"It's fine," Gus said. The ink on the comic book cover was now marred with smudged fingerprints. "It's just hard, you know?"

"Yeah. I do know. I know really, really well." Cooper put his arm around Gus's shoulder, and Gus slumped against his side. He didn't cry, but Cooper almost wished he would. He knew what to do with tears. He was used to Jess's. What he wasn't used to was the sense of utter defeat he felt in his friend.

"I will say, though," Cooper added, "when family stuff gets messy, sometimes being together is harder than staying apart. Maybe sending you here was your parents' way of sparing you some of the ugly stuff."

Gus shrugged.

"After our dad moved out, but before the divorce was final, Jess and I would have these . . . dates? . . . with my dad. They were *so* awkward. I remember this one time, after my dad hadn't seen us for, like, a month and a half, we met up with him at the park a few blocks over. He showed up with this cheap gas-station Frisbee, but he was still in a suit. He threw it around, and Jess, of course, ran after it like a puppy, while he stayed on this tiny patch of asphalt under the basketball hoop so his fancy leather shoes wouldn't get wet or muddy. I just sat on the swings, staring. I mean, *seriously*? You can't bother to change? He didn't even look at me, and then, after maybe forty minutes, tops, he checked his watch and informed us he had to go. Like the whole thing had been a real chore."

Gus stopped strangling his comic, took a deep breath, and sat up a little straighter. They watched cars go by, listening to the sounds of the city. Then, in a very quiet voice, Gus asked, "Do you ever feel like it's all your fault?"

"Only every day."

Gus half smiled and said, "But see, I don't get that for you. It seems super obvious that there's nothing that *you* did, or even could do, that would make a grown-up do the things your dad did. It doesn't make sense."

"You know I could say the exact same thing to you about your parents, right?"

"But I don't believe you," Gus said, now with a full grin.

"And I don't believe you!"

"Why are we like this?" Gus yelled good-humoredly to the sky, shaking both fists for emphasis, before looking nervously behind him toward Ms. Dreffel's window.

"I don't know," Cooper whispered yelled with the same fist gesture. "But, for the love of all that's holy, do *not* wake that old lady up!"

They both stiffled their laughs while anxiously watching the door. It stayed closed.

"You know," Gus said, "when I was packing to come here, I finally had to tell one of my friends what was going on with my family. I thought I was going to die of embarrassment, but then he ended up telling me his mom doesn't leave the house because she gets really freaked out around other people, and he somehow thinks it's because she's ashamed of *him*. And he said his uncle's this great guy in public, but he screams at his cousin if he leaves even a sock on the floor, so the kid blames himself for every one of his dad's explosions. And I know his cousin, he's this soccer star, super nice. But he still feels like a total failure because his dad's an ass."

"That's messed up."

"I know. But that's the thing. I could see their situations so clearly, and it made me wonder what *my* world looks like to them. From the outside. I've been trying to see my family through someone else's eyes. Anyone else's." Gus paused and crossed his arms tightly around himself.

"How's that going?" Cooper asked.

"Not great!" Gus laughed, but Cooper could tell he didn't think it was funny. "I mean, I keep telling myself that when my parents seem to have forgotten about me, maybe it isn't because *I'm* forgettable. I try to tell myself that maybe I'm not the problem, they are."

"They. Are." Cooper said. "None of this is your fault."

"Yeah, my brain gets it, but my heart doesn't. Right?"

Right. Cooper stared out at the street and was surprised to feel a clutch in his throat. Could he ever see his own family from the outside? To truly believe that it wasn't all his fault? When his father had left, Cooper kept telling himself that his dad needed to live some wildly different sort of life. Make a huge change. But then, his dad's life was pretty much the same as it had always been—the only difference being an entirely new cast of characters. It was impossible for Cooper to not to feel like he was the problem. He wiped his cheek with the back of his hand.

"Maybe, for now," Gus said, "it's enough that we believe it for each other?"

Cooper nodded slightly, trying the idea on for size.

"I'll go first. Cooper, it's not your fault."

Two more tears tracked down Cooper's face as he said, "It's not your fault, either."

25

"Hey," Cooper said to his mom as he entered the kitchen on the stroke of 5:30, just as he had promised Jess. The scent of garlic and onions made his stomach growl. "What's for dinner? It smells great in here."

"Shakshouka!" his mother said with a playful flourish.

Her lighthearted mood was a welcome shift after his conversation with Gus. "Shak-what-a?"

"Shakshouka! It's Israeli."

"Oh man," he said with a wry smile, "and I'd really been looking forward to eggs tonight."

His mother snapped the kitchen towel in his direction.

"Yolk's on you, buddy! It *does* have eggs, baked right on top."

"Noooooo," he moaned jokingly.

"Well, my little food critic, I guess you'll just have to start cooking dinner around here yourself if you want something different."

"Not gonna happen."

"Yes, I know." She laughed. "Hey, how's your homework coming along?"

"All done." Cooper got a glass of water and leaned against the sink. He hadn't seen his mom good-humored like this in a long time. "Do you want any help with dinner?"

His mother drew back in feigned shock. "Who are you, and what have you done with Cooper?" Cooper stuck his tongue out, which she returned before smiling again. "I do appreciate the offer, but this is basically done. All that's left is cracking the eggs and sticking it in the oven to bake."

"Where's Jess?" he asked.

"She's been upstairs for a while. She must have a lot of homework."

Cooper knew she had been almost finished when he left an hour ago. He downed his water and headed upstairs.

"Vigilantes Unum!" Jess hissed at Cooper as he walked into his room. She was exactly where he had left her on his bedroom floor an hour ago, scribbling notes and practically pounding on the iPad.

"Hmm, I know I've heard that phrase somewhere before," he joked, scratching his chin, before realizing that Jess was intensely serious.

"Cooper, close the door. I think we got it wrong. So, so wrong."

He did as he was told. "Got what wrong?"

"Elena! Her role in all of this. I got to thinking about *Vigilantes Unum,* and how 'vigilantes' must mean something different than what we thought, right? It can't mean to punish, not if Elena is a victim too. So, I tried searching for different meanings for the whole phrase. Both words are Latin, not just the unum part."

"Okay . . ." Cooper looked down at the notepad but couldn't make sense of all that she had scribbled there. "What does it mean, then?"

"Well, one translation is 'one watching.'"

"One watching?" Cooper repeated.

"Like, one who is watching over. One who protects. And I also researched more about ravens. In some cultures, yes, they're omens of danger, but in others, they're believed to *warn* against danger. They're even considered guardians of the Tower of London."

Cooper was trying to make sense of his sister's anxious energy. Nothing she had said so far contradicted what they already believed, yet worry was radiating from her. "So, that actually fits better with our theory, right? It only proves we're on the right track."

Jess shook her head vehemently, like she was frustrated with her own inability to get Cooper to see. She opened the iPad and turned it to him. "Park Cho."

"Park what?"

"Not what. Who! Park Cho," she repeated. "From the Sampoong Mall?"

"What about him?"

"Look." She pointed to the screen. "This article talks about him." She read aloud: "Park Cho told KBS-TV he was on the ground floor Thursday before the collapse. 'I felt a terrible quake, and then people began racing down from the upper floors.' I found a video clip of him being interviewed at the scene, and he was a kid! He was your age in 1995."

Jess navigated back to another article. "And at the Triangle fire, it talks about Beatrice Moretti, who was 'the last person known to leave work before the inferno began.'"

"And?" Cooper said.

"She had lied about her age to get the job. She was really twelve. In both of these articles, a kid left *right before* disaster struck."

"I don't get it."

"These are people who were seconds away from death, but somehow, right before everything happened, they were spared. Like someone had warned them."

Cooper began to see what his sister was trying to say. "Watching over them, even though so many others died."

"Watching over them and *only* them. And I found one more article about the Charfield crash we hadn't read before." Jess handed him the iPad.

Cooper skimmed the article while Jess read over his shoulder. He traced the text with a finger, mumbling words as he searched for anything that fit, and near the bottom, he read aloud:

On a day filled with seemingly endless sorrow, there was one small miracle that came to light late in the day's recovery efforts. Mr. and Mrs. Edward Hughes had arrived in the early morning hours at Charfield Station to receive their child, Geoffrey, who was returning from a visit with his aunt in Bristol. An anguished Mrs. Hughes had to be assisted back to her coach when it became inescapably clear that their son was not among the survivors. Hours later, however, a telegram arrived informing the Hughes family that their child had missed the train that morning and was, in fact, alive and well in Bristol.

"We were almost right," Jess said with fear in her eyes. "We did have things upside down and backward. But the accidents that we've found? They aren't the times Elena failed. They're the times that she's succeeded. Elena's never been able to save everyone. *Just one.*"

"*Unum,*" Cooper whispered.

"It doesn't mean 'one watching over.' It means 'watching over *ONE*.' That's the power she has," Jess said. "She can't stop the disasters. She dies in someone's place."

Cooper heard his pulse throbbing in his ears. Could Jess be right? Was this the truth they had been missing? The piece of the puzzle that Elena hadn't been able to tell him? He suddenly felt immensely foolish for believing that he, Jess, and Gus had any power over what the future brought. If Elena couldn't stop it, they certainly held no power to do so.

"She has died over and over again," said Jess. "She dies so one kid doesn't have to. *That* is her quest."

"And that's why she couldn't risk telling me what she does. If she'd told me that she only dies in the place of one . . ." He trailed off, sitting down hard onto his bed.

Jess sat next to him. ". . . that leaves two of us in serious trouble."

26

If the shakshouka was any good, Cooper wouldn't have been able to say. It tasted like paste as the reality of their situation crashed over Cooper again and again.

One of them was safe.

Two of them were not.

No wonder Elena wouldn't tell him anything more. How could she have looked him in the eye and told him two of their three were doomed? Them and so many more.

Cooper texted Gus Jess's *Vigilantes Unum* findings before going to bed, and Gus's only reply was:

That's not good.

What else was there to say?

Cooper walked through school the next day in a state of high alert, wondering if it was possible to feel any more paranoid. Zack dropped a folder in class, and the bang of it hitting the floor almost flattened Cooper. While everyone had laughed at his overreaction, Zack had asked, "Are you okay?"

"Yeah, yeah. I'm good." *Nope. Not at all.*

That afternoon, when Cooper and Jess came home, they were surprised to find their mom home early.

"Hey, Mom!" Jess said.

"What are you doing home?" Cooper said, spooked by any breach in the regular routine. He also didn't like the we-need-to-talk look in his mother's eye or the fact that she'd already changed out of her usual work clothes.

As Cooper lowered himself into a chair, he heard Jess's voice on the other side of the kitchen.

"Five, four, three, two, one, ouch!" *Pop-click.*

The noise was a familiar one—the click of a finger lancet. Cooper watched as Jess stood at the kitchen counter, squeezing a drop of blood onto the test strip of her glucometer. "One forty-five, Mom," she turned and announced a few seconds later. She giggled at the look on Cooper's face and shrugged.

Cooper blinked. He hadn't even thought of Jess's diabetes in the past three weeks. In all those days of living on the other side of the house, she had had to figure it out on her own. And she had. He gave her a little thumbs-up that she returned.

"Jess, come have a seat," their mother said.

Jess's expression changed at these words. The last time Mom had asked them to have a seat, it was because Dad was having yet another kid. She crept to a chair and perched halfway on its edge, poised to bolt.

"I wanted to ask you guys a question," Mom continued.

"Okay," Cooper said, though it didn't feel okay at all.

Their mother shifted in her seat and sat up a little straighter. "You know it's been a few years since your father and I split up."

Not a question, Cooper thought. He didn't like how this was starting, and there wasn't much more he could take at the moment.

"Yeah . . . ?" said Jess.

Mom folded her hands in front of her. They were like a mashup from two completely different people: their backs had skin like parched desert sand, with fissures and cracking lines, and her fingernails were rough, dry, and almost always stained from pottery clay. But her palms were soft and smooth from hours immersed in massage oil, giving comfort and calm to others.

"Guys," she said. "I miss having an adult I can share

things with. A partner. I've met a very nice person at the arts center who has asked me out to dinner."

Jess's mouth dropped open.

"I would like to go, but I knew we had to talk about it before I could say yes."

The chair beneath Jess shot back as she stood and spat, "But what about Dad?"

Their mother's shoulders sagged slightly, but before she could speak, Cooper stepped in.

"Jess—" he started.

She shot him a disgusted glare and yelled, "What? You're okay with this?"

"Dad's *married*, Jess. There is no Dad in this equation."

"He needs more time!" Jess yelled at her mother, as if Dad, too, were trapped in some chrysalis, trying to get out. "He'll never come back if you do this!"

"Oh, honey," their mother sighed. "He's never coming back either way."

"You don't know that!"

"Yes, Jess. I do. I think we *all* do."

With that, Jess ran upstairs and slammed her bedroom door. Cooper and his mom sat staring at each other, their heavy breaths rising and falling in sync.

"I knew she'd be upset," she finally said. "But I didn't think . . ."

"Yeah," Cooper said. "Jess still has hopes."

After a quiet moment, Mom said, "What about you?"

Cooper looked at his mother in shock. "Mom, I gave up hoping on Dad a long time ago."

"No," she said with a small laugh. "I mean, what do you think about me going out to dinner?"

"Oh."

He didn't know what he thought. He knew his mom used to have an energy that fueled their family with excitement and wonder at the world around them, but he hadn't seen that side of her in a long time. He knew there were nights when she cried quietly in her room, and she seemed so tired all the time, even when she had a break from work. It was almost like she'd forgotten how to wake up all the way. He'd always assumed she was exhausted by anger and disappointment, the same way he was. But sitting, looking at her now, he realized maybe part of it was loneliness.

"Coop, I don't *need* to do this. I love you and your sister. You're my everything. But . . . I want to go to dinner with Eric. I want to have someone to share happiness with, someone my own age. I'm ready for that again."

"Is he more like you?" Cooper asked.

His mom tipped her head. "What do you mean? More like me than your dad was?"

Cooper nodded slightly. "You and Dad are so . . .

253

different from each other. Like, opposite."

"Believe it or not, those differences were a big part of why we fell in love in the first place. We complemented each other. I made him more carefree, he made me more grounded. And the parts that didn't fit? Well, they didn't seem to matter so much back then." She stared at the floor with a melancholy smile. Then, with a sigh, she looked Cooper squarely in the eye and said, "Or maybe we were better at pretending they weren't there."

"So. Is this new guy more like you?"

"Yeah, sweetie. He is."

Cooper slowly pushed his chair out and stood. His mom stayed still, her hands clasped tightly in front of her, waiting. He leaned a millimeter forward, then a few more. Then he took a step toward his mother and held his arms out.

His mom's eyes crinkled as she stood and wrapped her arms around him. They hugged for what felt like hours, as if Cooper was back on In-Between time. His mother's soft hands rubbed his back, over and over, as if she were making up for all the times in the last year that it hadn't happened. That he hadn't *let* it happen. Something in Cooper's chest unclenched.

He finally murmured into her shoulder, "Mom, I just want you to be happy."

She pulled back and took him gently by the shoulders.

Her eyes were shiny. "I want you to be happy too, Coop."

He looked her right in the eye. Maybe he was much, much more like his mom than he'd ever realized. Maybe she wasn't the only one struggling to remember what it was like to wake up.

Cooper's mother made them both warm cups of tea, and they sat in the kitchen, blowing and sipping in a comfortable quiet. When the last drop was gone, Cooper's mom turned to him. "Do you mind if I go for a ride? I'm going to need some time to figure out how to talk to Jess about all this."

"Yeah, go. We'll be fine."

"Thanks, bud." His mother gave him another quick hug and went to her room to change into her biking gear.

Cooper grabbed his backpack and went up to his room, figuring he'd do his homework and give his sister a little space. He was working his first math problem when Jess walked into his room, crossed to his bed, and sat on its edge, her face shrouded by her long hair.

Cooper waited for her to say something but ultimately put his pencil down and turned in his chair. He rested his folded arms on the chair's back, his chin atop his hand. "You okay?"

"He's never coming back, is he?" she whispered.

Cooper had told her his thoughts on this more times

than he could count, imploring Jess to see the truth. But something about this moment—her posture, her voice—told Cooper she was ready to truly hear it for the first time.

"No," he said.

He watched as the word struck her across the face, hurting them both.

"No," she repeated softly. She uttered it a few more times, as if testing its weight. Then she lifted her chin toward the ceiling. She looked like she was trying not to cry, then her face screwed up in anger. "But we were here first!" she said.

"I know." Cooper agreed that he and Jess should have some sort of cosmic priority as Dr. Stewart's first-born children, not these latecomers. "We were, but it doesn't matter."

"You mean *we* don't matter."

He had no response to that. He'd been feeling the searing heat of this same conclusion for years now, but after his conversation with Gus, he wondered if they were both wrong. They all mattered, all three of them, at least to one another.

"Jess, what Dad's done . . . I don't think I'll ever understand it or get over it. But we have to keep living our lives, and we can't take it out on Mom. She's the one who's always been here. Who always will be."

"But a *date*?"

"Yes, a date."

"You're seriously cool with that?"

Cooper waited until Jess looked at him before saying, "What I'm cool with is Mom being happy. If going out to dinner with this Eric guy makes her happy, then isn't that worth it?"

"I do *not* want a new dad!"

Cooper walked to the bed and sat down with his arm around his sister's shoulder. "Jess, it's a date, not a wedding."

"But what if she ends up liking him? Like *really* liking him? What do we do then?"

This possibility sounded awful to Cooper as well, but he said, "If she likes him that much, maybe it's because he's really likable. Maybe we'd like him too."

"Nope." Jess shook her head.

"Okay, fine. You don't have to like him. To be honest, I'm not even asking *myself* to like him, or the next him or even the next after that."

Jess shot him an angry side-eye. "Enough already!"

Cooper laughed and pulled her tighter. "What I am trying to say is that what we think isn't what really matters. What matters is if *Mom* likes him. She's lonely, Jess. Lonely in a way I don't think you and I can fix." When Jess said nothing, he added, "You know that we are always Mom's first priority, right? No date will ever change that."

Jess tucked her hair behind her ears and slowly lifted her

gaze to look straight at Cooper. "Are you *sure*?"

"I'm positive, and you can be too. She's not Dad."

Jess exhaled. It was a long, slow release. She then chewed on her bottom lip and began to pick at the cuticle on her thumb. "Okay. But I'm still gonna have to think about it . . . about this *Eric*."

That was fair. It was a lot to take in.

This time—unlike the time with Gus weeks ago—the moment the idea popped into Cooper's head, he knew it felt right. "There's something I want to show you. Something cool."

"Oh yeah?" She didn't smile, but Cooper could tell he'd caught her interest.

"Yeah. Come on. We're going out."

"Where?"

"You'll see."

"Is it safe?"

"Honestly, I have no idea anymore."

Jess looked at him for a second but then stood up. "Okay. Let me get my coat from my room."

Yes. Jess would make an excellent bridge screamer.

27

"I should do *what?*" Jess asked from her spot on the bridge. Cooper hadn't told her anything until they were standing in yelling position, and she clearly now thought her brother had a screw loose.

"Just let it out. Let all of it out."

Jess instead scanned all the people in the cars creeping slowly past in rush-hour traffic, one eyebrow creeping up her forehead.

"No one cares, Jess. I don't think anyone can even hear you."

"Okay, I'll do it, but you first."

"Sure." Cooper grabbed the railing and let out a scream.

It was loud enough that, for the first time, he saw a passenger in the nearest car glance at him with concern. Cooper simply waved with a grin.

"I thought you said they couldn't hear." Jess laughed nervously.

"Maybe they can when traffic's slow like this," he said with a shrug. "Who cares?"

Jess put one hand on the rail, and with her other hand she reached out to her brother. He took it and squeezed. Then she let loose perhaps the loudest scream he'd ever heard on the bridge.

"Nice!" he said after she finished and turned to him with a look of great satisfaction. "You're a natural."

They each took their turns, screaming until they were breathless. Cooper felt lighter with each yell, but he had also arrived with less weight than usual. Jess's yells, in contrast, were raw. Angry. It wasn't something Cooper was accustomed to in his little sister. There was a lot more power packed into her than he'd realized.

When they were both screamed out, the comfortable calm that always followed settled over both of them.

"How often do you come down here?" Jess said, overlooking the city.

"Whenever I'm so angry I don't know what to do with myself."

"So, all the time?" she said with a grin.

"Basically." But even as he said this, something within him shifted. For over three years, anger had been a daily companion, but standing here with Jess, he felt like maybe he had screamed all he needed to about his family. The well had run dry. He looked around at the old bridge, with its cracked cement and rusted-out railings, and wondered if this was, perhaps, the last time he would come here.

"Hey, guys!"

Cooper was the first to turn at the sound of the voice, faintly coming from their left. But it was Jess who said, "Is that Gus?"

He was running toward them from the south side of the bridge, unmistakable in his same sweatshirt, one arm waving, one clutching his journal. There was an urgency on his face that only added to Cooper's anxiety at the three of them being together, in one place, for the first time in weeks. It was against the plan.

Jess must have felt the same. "Should I head home?" she asked.

Before Cooper could answer, Gus reached them, winded, and put his hands on his knees. "Hey!" he said. "You weren't home, so I thought I might find you here."

Cooper turned to his sister. "Wait for me at the light," he said, pointing in the distance to the intersection behind

261

Gus, the first turnoff toward home.

Jess began to leave, but Gus held up a hand to stop her. "No. Stay. This will only take a second, I promise."

"Okay . . ." Cooper looked back and forth between Jess and Gus. Traffic was at a near standstill, and exhaust fumes filled the air around them.

"I know we said we'd stay apart, but I needed to find you guys . . . to say goodbye."

"What?" both Cooper and Jess said together.

Gus pushed himself upright. "Yeah. The good news is that our whole staying-apart plan just got a lot easier. The bad news is that, apparently, I'm heading back home today."

Cooper was speechless. He had always known Gus would go back to Oklahoma, back to his parents, at some point. He was never planning to live with his grandmother forever. Cooper just hadn't considered it could be so soon.

"But what about school?" Jess said.

"Yeah, you can't leave midsemester," Cooper said, even as he knew how ridiculous his words sounded, as if no one had ever left in the middle of the year. But his mind was spinning around the true reason for his distress: that he needed Gus here, he needed his friendship. He couldn't lose someone important again. Instead he said, "I mean, have your parents even worked things out yet?"

"I can't really tell," Gus said with a sad laugh. "But my

grandma is *done* playing parent. It's gonna be okay, though."
It sounded like he was trying to convince himself as much
as Cooper and Jess.

"If your parents are never around, what do they care if
you stay here? You could move in with us!" Cooper's mom's
words echoed in his mind: *I want to have someone to share
happiness with.* "If you go home, you're going to be so . . .
alone."

"Yeah. But it's okay, Coop," Gus said. "I wish I didn't
have to go either, but I'm glad I was here for a while, at least.
That we actually got to know each other. It's been a long
time since . . . well, I don't know if I've ever had friends like
you guys."

Cooper's throat tightened and his eyes burned. He nodded at Gus's words, agreeing with them down to his toes.

"So. I should go," Gus said and took a few slow steps
away. Jess ran over to him and enveloped him in a hug,
which Gus returned fiercely, but Cooper found he couldn't
move. No words, no hugs. Every fiber of him refused to
participate in this farewell.

Gus appeared to understand. He offered Cooper a warm
smile and small wave before turning and walking away.

"So, is it over then?" Jess said quietly.

It took Cooper a moment to understand what she meant.
He had almost forgotten about Elena, about the impending

disaster. And in that moment, he almost didn't care. All he really wanted was for his friend to stay, no matter the risk.

"This sucks," Cooper whispered. He turned away and ran his fingers through his hair. This wasn't the kind of hurt that made Cooper want to scream and rage over the river. Instead he felt drained. Empty.

It was then that a crack, like the sound of a ball on a bat, shot through the air.

The sound came from under their feet. Cooper's and Jess's eyes snapped downward.

"What was that?" Jess asked, her voice thin. "Did someone get rear-ended or something?"

Cooper didn't answer. He couldn't. Because he was looking toward the end of the bridge.

At *her*.

Coming toward them from the north, her white-blond hair whipping in the wind, was Elena. Her *Vigilantes* shield shimmered brightly in the afternoon sunlight. The red of the raven's eye and the swords' hilts glowed intensely.

Jess gasped, "Oh no."

Both Jess and Cooper whipped around to see that, though Gus was far from them, he was still on the bridge, walking south.

They were all here together. The time was now.

Disaster had finally come for them.

28

"**R**un!" Cooper yelled as he and his sister took off after Gus. How had they let this happen? They had been safe for weeks by staying apart.

Cooper looked ahead, hoping that Gus had already gotten off the bridge, but instead was horrified to see his friend walking back toward them.

"Gus!" Cooper yelled. "Turn around! Get off the bridge!"

Another *CRACK* shot out, and though there was no movement accompanying these sounds, it was followed by the slow sighing creak of metal bending against its will.

Cooper streaked past car after car, realizing with dread that none of the people inside the cars, their radios or phones blaring, had heard the ominous sounds. So many vehicles, each firmly locked in rush-hour traffic. Could he knock on every window and convince all of them they were in great danger? How much time did they have?

As if in response, a third loud report came, this time with a violent shudder.

"Gus!" Cooper said as they met. "Turn around!" Both he and Jess tried to grab Gus's arms, to pull him along with them. But Gus managed to shake them both off and continue his march toward Elena.

Cooper pulled up to go back for his friend, but Gus yelled, "Keep going! Both of you, get off the bridge." There was a calm, steady determination in Gus's words. Cooper watched the distance between them grow as a few drivers opened their doors and stood up to assess the situation. Fear clutched at his chest. What was Gus trying to do?

A plan hatched in Cooper's mind. He held his ground and shouted, "Elena!" as another gut-twisting shudder rocked the bridge. "You don't have to do this! All of us, all *four* of us, can get off this bridge. Please!"

Elena had now reached the middle of the bridge, the spot where Cooper had spent so many hours, and Gus continued until he was right in front of her. Then Elena rested her hands on his shoulders and looked him in the eye, saying something only he could hear.

"No one has to die!" Cooper howled against the wind. "Come with us now! We can *all* be safe!"

Then Gus turned and looked squarely at Cooper. He drew his arm back and flung his journal in a high arc toward Cooper, its brilliant white pages fluttering like a hundred-winged butterfly. Cooper caught it, pages splayed.

A chill tickled at the back of his neck, a rising sense of dread. Between his fingers, he saw the heading of each page.

Dearest Mother,

"Oh no," Cooper uttered with full understanding, all fight in him now gone.

Gus pulled at the sleeve of his sweatshirt, removing one arm and then the other. He lifted the garment up and over his head, and Jess gasped. Cooper didn't know if he felt unsteady because of the shaking cement under his feet or from his world being knocked off its axis.

Beneath Gus's sweatshirt was a white V-neck T-shirt, with a golden emblem stitched to the chest. A raven clutching a banner.

"No," Cooper uttered, shaking his head. This couldn't be the answer. It had been right in front of them all along.

I'm heading back home, Gus had said. *It's gonna be okay. Of course.*

My sister's out in the living world right now, on a quest, Elena had told him. Cooper had simply assumed Elena meant somewhere else, some other city, some other tragedy.

Cooper felt lightheaded as so many memories began exploding in his mind: Gus alone at the bus stop. Gus sitting in no-man's-land in row three. The moment Zack had sat down next to him in the lunchroom. *Sorry to leave you alone like that.*

Ms. Dreffel had screamed at Cooper and Jess that day on her porch as if no one had entered her home in years. That was because no one had. Gus didn't live at Ms. Dreffel's. He lived down the hall from Elena, in that second messy bedroom, invisible to everyone but Cooper and Jess.

Gus took Elena's hand, a mirror image of Cooper and Jess.

Two lives for two lives. It made so much more sense.

Then Gus flickered. For a moment so brief Cooper wasn't sure he saw it, a girl with long braids and a familiar smile stood beside Elena. She wore a heavy woolen coat and a kind expression. It was unmistakably Gus behind her eyes. Then the Gus that Cooper knew reappeared.

Jess cried out in surprise. Cooper shouted out to them one more time. "Please! Don't do this. Both of you, come with us!"

"This is the way it works," Elena said calmly, her voice

carrying over the distance unnaturally. "The *only* way it works."

"Go," Gus said, nodding.

"No . . . ," Cooper said, the word dying on his lips. Another cracking sound filled the air, but it was accompanied with a flash that emanated from Gus and Elena themselves, bright as lightning. Both Cooper and Jess had to turn away, shielding their eyes, but when they peered again at Gus and Elena, there was a slight glow to their outlines. They appeared more solidly rooted where they stood, and their colors were more vivid, more saturated.

Some people had begun to get out of their cars and run for the ends of the bridge, and they yelled at Elena and Gus to run as they did. Everyone could see the blond girl and the kind boy with the matching crests now. They would be found among the rubble. After.

I'm glad I was here for a while, Cooper heard, and he didn't know if Gus said it now or if Gus's words from earlier were echoing in his mind. The final word was punctuated by the loudest bang yet, and the bridge quaked with such force that Jess had to reach out to the handrail to stay on her feet. The angle of the sidewalk tipped forward with a horrifying lurch. The sounds of car doors opening and the distressed cries of dozens of people, began to fill the air. The truth of what was happening was now undeniable.

"This isn't your future anymore," Elena said, louder but still calm. "It's ours."

With a hefty tug from Jess, Cooper started to move, but not before one last shared glance with Gus. His friend nodded gravely.

Cooper turned and ran as fast as he could. Tears streamed down his face, fueled by terror, confusion, and heartbreak.

The crumbling began. The northern edge of the bridge tore away from its land-secured moorings, ripping free as if it were a piece of notebook paper. The highway, along with the cars on it, began to fall.

Jess and Cooper both screamed as they ran south, faster, faster. Cooper gripped the binding of the journal so hard it bent. Even as they closed in on the end of the bridge, it still appeared terrifyingly far away.

The bridge collapsed in sections, one support beam at a time, into the river below. With each chunk, Cooper could hear catastrophe gaining on them from behind, the metal struts beneath them buckling and screaming more loudly with each step. He wanted to cover his ears and his eyes to shut out the horror of what was happening. Many people had made it off the bridge, but so many were still trapped. Why couldn't he and Jess somehow save them all? Why did he deserve to live when so many others wouldn't?

"Faster!" Jess yelled. Cooper heard the segment of bridge directly behind them give way, the unearthly din of fracturing cement and wrenching beams only slightly louder in Cooper's ears than his heaving breaths.

We're not going to make it! his mind screamed.

Then, as if a strong wind had come up behind them, they moved forward faster than their legs should have carried them. Cooper felt like he had when he was learning how to ride a bike and his dad had gently placed a hand on his back to propel him forward. He and Jess reached the next bridge section at the moment that the section they'd been on fell away. This new slab, incredibly, began to shift upward, like a giant asphalt teeter-totter, until the tilt became so steep that gravity took over. Jess cried out, and Cooper felt certain his heart was going to burst from its bony cage as they fell and started sliding forward.

They skidded thirty or so feet on the surface of the asphalt before coming to rest firmly against the front bumper of a car. There was a final, colossal crashing, splashing sound before an eerie quiet descended, made all the more notable by two distant car horns, blaring on the other riverbank.

Just like that, it was over.

They were sitting fifty feet below where they'd been moments earlier, the southern tip of this slab of the bridge having come to rest on the south bank of the river. A row of trees and a small frontage road stretched to either side of Cooper and Jess.

"Are you okay?" Cooper said.

Jess nodded, tears having cut tracks down her face. "I think so."

With bloodied hands and ripped pants, they stood. Their section of the bridge now lay bent in two, like a giant letter L, part aiming straight up for the sky, still buttressed by metal that hadn't failed, and part flat on the river's shoulder. A crumpled elbow of rubble lay between. The slab they had escaped seconds before the tilt now lay crumpled in the river.

Jess offered Cooper a hand, and they each stepped carefully as they moved around debris and damaged cars toward solid land.

"Are you kids okay?" a man asked, helping them down to a patch of grass. He had blood coming from a cut on his forehead.

"Yeah. I think so," Jess said again.

Once they stood on the riverbank, Cooper and Jess walked far enough to the side to see the entirety of the disaster. What they saw defied belief. Much of the bridge was in the river, and cars were scattered all around like a child's Matchbox set that had been thrown in a tantrum. The smells of motor oil, gasoline, and smoke clogged the air. A huge chunk of road lay mangled on the opposite riverbank, similar to theirs, and other sections still dangled from support beams at terrifying angles.

Jess buried her face in Cooper's side. He put an arm around her, wishing there was someone bigger yet, beside him, who he could bury his face against.

The stillness lasted for a minute or so before sound and motion erupted everywhere. Shouting, sirens, crying.

Cooper and Jess, however, remained stock-still, side by side, watching it all.

Finally Jess said, "They're gone, aren't they?"

"Yeah," Cooper whispered. "They are."

Unidentified, all over again.

29

They hadn't saved Elena. Or Gus.

Elena and Gus were back in the In-Between now, either awakening to the next tragedy or . . .

Cooper felt a hole open in his chest at the thought of both of their fate. He needed to believe, as he watched the dust and smoke rise from the rubble, that there was some way it was going to be okay. Maybe this time, that gilded door in the In-Between would unlock—maybe it would open and finally allow Elena and Gus through. Surely they had done enough to finally be granted passage to their parents in the Beyond.

But why would this time be any different? Elena and Gus had done their job. Enter, die, return. And repeat. And repeat.

Cooper and Jess had changed nothing.

Jess slowly turned away from the scene before them and muttered, "We should go home."

Cooper took one last look at the void above the river that should have held a bridge, and a taste of bile filled the back of his throat. He felt heavy with the weight of failure, helplessness, and loss. Not only had he failed Elena and Gus, he hadn't been able to save any of the others on the bridge. All those other people. It was staggering.

They had only walked half a block before Cooper had to put his hands on his knees to steady himself against a wave of emotion that bent him in half. He cried. Unrestrained, unfettered, and unabashed. He cried for all the people who had still been on the bridge, for Jess and all she had been through, for Elena and the sacrifice she'd made *again*. For Gus, his best friend.

Jess came to her brother's side and put an arm around him. Cooper clutched his way up to her shoulders, wrapped his arms around her neck, and buried his face. He put some of this impossible weight on her. She held it just fine.

Jess hugged him and gently smoothed the back of his

hair with one hand, the way he had done for her so many times before. She didn't say *Shhhh, there there* or *It's okay.* It wasn't okay. How could it ever be okay?

"We were never in control of any of it, Jess," Cooper said. The bridge, his parents' divorce, Jess's diabetes . . . there were endless aspects in his life where Cooper and Jess didn't get a say. His knees buckled as these thoughts threatened to crush him. Jess held fast.

When he finally pulled away from his sister, she tipped her head toward Gus's journal, still in Cooper's grip. "I think we should read it."

"I . . . I don't know if I can."

"He gave it to us for a reason." Jess gently pulled Cooper down to sit on the curb and took the book. She held it on her lap and ran her hand over the cover that had been half worn away during its slide down the asphalt.

Cooper didn't stop Jess from opening the journal, but he turned away. "He knew all along. All this time, Gus knew all the answers."

Jess began flipping through the pages of the journal. "Cooper, all of these entries are like that letter you found, and look at this." Inside the cover, against the binding, were the frayed remains of multiple pages that had been torn out. "It's the same handwriting. It was never Elena at all. That letter was written by Gus."

Cooper nodded.

Jess thumbed through dozens of entries, some detailing events as far back as the 1800s, from Peru, California, and Tibet. Japan, Canada, and Australia. Letter after letter detailed tragedies they had never found.

"That day Gus said he was calling his grandma from our driveway," Jess said slowly, the truth dawning, "he didn't call Ms. Dreffel. He called Elena, didn't he? He must have told her we were starting to figure things out, because she wouldn't say a word to us after that. She slammed the door in your face and never sat on the swing again."

Gus had tied an intricate knot, and Cooper realized it was going to take them a long time to unravel all the threads. The phone call, the bus rides, their lunch in Mrs. Wishingrad's room . . . So many clues to the truth they had both missed.

Suddenly Jess smacked both hands down on the open pages. "Cooper, here's one in England!" She quickly ran her finger over the text. "It's from 1928. This must be the train." She traced the lines with her finger as she read aloud, hopping to keywords and phrases in the narrative:

"'A bittersweet quest . . . I'd never been back home. Lamplighters, sidecar motorbikes, automobiles . . . Bristol Temple Meads Station!' This is it, Coop! The train that crashed in Charfield was from Bristol." She read on, now more thoroughly:

"My heart fell as I saw him. The young boy in a crisp little suit and hat was being pushed past me by a rather insistent older woman. The child was unmistakably vivid and corporeal. He was my quest.

"The urgency coursed through me; my duty was undeniably imminent. We had spent three months on our mission in Pyongyang, five months in the Algerian Sahara Desert. Why, oh why, now that I was on my home soil, was I acting within moments of arrival? I looked around the bustling crowds and shimmering shops of my home country, wanting to cry.

"The woman tugged at the boy, accusing him of dawdling, though he hauled a heavy suitcase and was moving as quickly as he could manage. He had a flushed face and damp brow despite the chill, and he begged the woman to let him rest for a moment, but she didn't even slow, saying, 'Geoffrey! Your parents will be awaiting you in Charfield. My sister will be furious with me if you miss this train.'

"I followed them into the station and waited. The woman counted out bills at the ticket desk while Geoffrey sat slumped on his bag. A massive sign overhead announced the train would be leaving from platform twelve in twenty minutes. I slipped past the many unseeing

278

eyes and followed the sign to all trains, though I wouldn't have needed any signage to know which terminus was mine; a brilliant green passenger train stood amidst ten or so faded and ghostly engines.

"Five minutes later, Geoffrey and his aunt approached a conductor, who checked his ticket and directed them one car down. At the door, the dour woman gave the boy a crisp nod before he climbed aboard and disappeared from view. She then stepped away from the train, straight-backed, both hands clutching her bag, and waited.

"Adults make my job so much harder than necessary.

"I consulted the large clock hanging above the platform. I would need to wait until the last possible moment.

"More passengers loaded, but I kept my eyes down, rolling a pebble with the toe of my shoe. Even though I know there is nothing I can do to save these people, I still try not to look at the faces of the doomed. A few last-minute passengers hurried aboard as the conductor shouted his final warnings.

"It was time.

"Being invisible can be lonely, but it certainly helps when you need to board a train without a ticket. I beat the conductor to the stairs and slipped past a man placing his bag in the overhead bin. Geoffrey was sitting in the back, thankfully in a seat without a window. If he'd seen his aunt—who was quietly and serenely awaiting his departure—it would have ruined everything.

"I ran up to him and told him that his aunt had sent me to fetch him; he needed to collect his bag and exit the train, something about today being the wrong day for him to travel. He looked alarmed as the train lurched slightly and began creeping forward, an inch at a time. I told him his aunt had realized she had made a mistake and his parents wouldn't be in Charfield to receive him. We were moving at a crawl as he scrambled to grab his things, barely even looking at me. He tossed his bag down and jumped to the platform, stumbling slightly on landing.

"I hurried to a window, relieved to see that his aunt was distractedly chatting with an older gentleman beside her. It wasn't until we had picked up quite a bit of speed that she noticed Geoffrey returning to her side. Her initial surprise gave way to frantic and futile gestures to stop the train. I watched the old woman berate poor Geoffrey as the train took its first turn, and they slipped out of sight.

"I sat down and watched the landscape flicker by through the window. All I had left to do was wait for the inevitable, knowing that by the time Geoffrey and *his family learned the terrible fate of this train, I would already be back in the In-Between."*

"Oh, Gus," Jess sighed.

Cooper shook his head. Every inch of him ached, imagining what it was like to be Gus, knowing that he was about to meet a terrible end. Even if he was going to wake up again.

Jess continued to flip through the pages of the journal. "And here's South Korea, 1995." She started to read aloud Gus's account of finding a boy they now knew was Park Cho at the Sampoong Mall, but Cooper told her to stop. He couldn't hear any more.

"Do you think it's possible that it's over?" he said.

Jess looked at him sideways. "Of course it's over. The bridge fell."

"No. I mean for Elena and Gus."

"Oh." Jess sighed. After a moment, she quietly added, "Is it terrible for me to hope so? I mean, even if they never make it through that door to their parents, if it's *truly* over—if they really died this time—at least they don't have to suffer anymore."

Cooper nodded. He stayed quiet as Jess finished skimming through the journal, flipping all the way to the end. He jumped slightly as Jess gripped his arm. "Coop. Look."

At the top of the last entry, instead of the same "Dearest Mother" that headed all the rest, Cooper saw "To my friends, Cooper and Jess."

He grabbed the journal and began reading Gus's final words.

30

To my friends, Cooper and Jess,

    *Today's the day. Elena and I will do exactly what
we've been destined to do ever since we stepped out of the
In-Between and into your world.*

    If you are reading this, of course, you already know that.

    *What you don't know is how different this particular
quest was for me. For so long, I have longed to know why
we save the people we do. Why we see you, your sister, and
the others as clear as day, while others succumb to the same
disasters that take us. It has dogged me, haunted me even.
There had to be a point, a purpose, to how these tragedies
played out. You have helped me finally understand.*

This quest started as unusually as it will end. Elena and I fought bitterly the day we arrived behind your house. I insisted we speak to you, try to understand your lives so we might understand our own. The people we save have always been ignorant of our work, but with our number of quests dwindling, I had to find answers before we died our final deaths.

This was not the first time Elena and I had argued about making contact, but she again forbade it, saying the risk was too great; that it could prevent us from being able to save you when we needed to, or keep you from being where you should be, or any number of unpredictable eventualities.

So I ran away.

I left the yellow house and spent the first few months here in Chicago wandering parks and alleys, staying away from Elena. We can feel when disaster is near, so I knew I had time, but Elena watched over you two like a hawk, perched on her swing, preventing me from interacting with either of you.

I, however, refused to take no for an answer. Elena never thought I'd be so bold as to board your bus or sit at your lunch table at school with you. I must admit, I was quite proud of myself that day the three of us met

284

in the alleyway, shamelessly flaunting that I'd already befriended you. Elena had no power to stop me once she realized I'd made contact.

But Elena was right about one thing—it was selfish of me to involve you, knowing what was going to happen. I was so blinded by my need for answers, for my hunger to fill the black holes of my knowledge, that I missed an obvious and terrible complication: that we would become true friends.

I am so sorry. I never meant for this to cause either of you any pain.

I hope it comes as some solace, however, that I now understand—and Cooper, you were the key. When you walked straight into the In-Between, Elena and I were gob-smacked. It simply wasn't possible! You hadn't, after all, left the living world the way we had. I couldn't guess how it was possible. But I now think I know. It was that story about your dad at the movie theater. You told me, "He just turned and walked out the door, like he hadn't seen me at all."

Elena and I have been wrong this whole time, think-ing the In-Between was only about being stuck between life and death. It's more than that. The In-Between's doors are open to anyone who is invisible. Anyone who feels for-gotten.

285

My friends, please know this now and forever: no matter how much your father, or anyone else, makes you feel otherwise, you are seen. You are brilliantly visible. Your pain and your loneliness are real, as are your kindness, your courage, and your sense of humor. You are not forgotten. And now that you have the chance to live, please, refuse to fade away.

Cooper, those stories I told you, of my friends back home? Those weren't lies; they're stories I gathered about other kids at your school, invisible as I was. They are the lives of your classmates, some of whom feel as forgotten as you and I do. Find them. See them the way you saw me.

If there's one thing Elena and I have learned over these decades, it's that bad things happen that no one can stop: divorce, illness, lost friendship, family heartbreak, and these awful, awful catastrophes. They, sadly, are part of being alive.

But so are joy, love, and happiness. These are things Elena and I missed out on when our lives ended too soon. So please, find those too. Make our sacrifice worth it.

You are not invisible. You are both unforgettable. Never doubt that.

Love,

Gus (and Elena)

P.S. Oh, and Cooper, I'm sorry I had to stretch the truth about my parents. They were always traveling, as Elena told you, just not in the way I had led you to believe.

Cooper gently closed the journal and clutched it to his chest. Neither he nor Jess spoke for a long while.

Invisible.

Repeating that word in his mind made a lump rise in Cooper's throat. It was so dead-on. So right. Those nine little letters encompassed everything Cooper had felt for the last few years, though he was quite certain he had never written that word in his journal. Funny how you can miss something so simple. So basic. It was the word that lived beneath all the rest.

Jess, her voice quiet, broke into his thoughts. "I still love him."

"Who? Dad?"

She nodded slowly.

"I know," Cooper said. "I think I do too. That's what makes this all so hard."

After a moment, Jess added, "Do we have to stop?"

Cooper thought for a moment, then shook his head. "No, I don't think so." He turned to his sister, and she looked so clear, so vivid, just like Elena and Gus had in their final seconds. "But maybe we can start seeing each other a little better too."

Jess appeared to try the idea on for size. "Deal."

Cooper stood and helped Jess up. The sky was the color of a deep bruise as they resumed their walk home. They moved away from the symphony of sirens swarming the area, their blare in sharp contrast to the soft crunch of leaves under Cooper's and Jess's feet. An ambulance flew by. They seemed to be the only people in the city who weren't rushing toward the bridge.

"I can't believe they're gone," Jess said, her breath making little wisps of steam in the cool air.

"I know." Cooper let out a long breath. "It's so unfair."

"It's kind of funny how the two of them argued, right?" Jess said. "That part about him refusing to do what his sister wanted him to do? Sounded kinda familiar."

"I guess it proves that sisters have been annoying throughout the centuries."

Jess gently punched Cooper on the shoulder. He smiled.

"They save people over and over again," Jess said, "but no one gets to save them."

"At least they have each other," Cooper said, but it wasn't much comfort. "Two sisters, whoever they truly are, back in the In-Between—"

With this thought, a realization exploded in Cooper's mind.

"Wait!"

He said it so loudly Jess jumped slightly. "What?"

"Could that be it? Is that how we save them too?"

Jess shook her head. "But Coop, it's already too late."

"For the bridge, yes! I mean to save them for forever! Come on!" Cooper took off running. If he was right, he knew how to open that golden door to their parents, out of the In-Between and into the Beyond.

Because something else *was* different this time, something that even Gus hadn't realized.

Cooper closed his eyes for a moment as he ran, hoping that they weren't already one death too late.

31

Cooper ran even faster than he had on the bridge. He streaked down the roads he and Jess had traveled an hour and a half earlier. It didn't seem possible that their entire world could be flipped upside-down in such a small amount of time.

Jess, arms pumping, pulled up beside Cooper. "What is it?" She spoke one breathless word at a time as they sprinted.

"I have to go back. Back into the In-Between!"

Jess fell back a few paces. "What? How?"

"I don't know, but I have to try!" Elena had told him that she and her sister had landed in the In-Between because they weren't missed by one single *living* soul. Because they'd been forgotten by everyone left behind.

That was what was different this time. *That* was something they had changed.

But Cooper needed one crucial piece of information.

Jess gained on him as they rounded a turn. "I'm coming too."

Cooper looked at his sister. Her head was held high, and there was a confidence in the square of her shoulders and the clarity of her gaze, even as they ran.

He smiled at her and she returned it. "Okay then," he said. "Let's do this."

They continued, side by side, taking the turn down the alley and toward their home. When Elena's house came into view, Cooper stumbled to a halt, and his mouth fell open.

The yellow house was gone. In its place, the abandoned building, complete with its yard of dirt and trash, was back.

"Oh no," Jess said, her gaze bouncing between the house and her brother. "Can we even get into the In-Between anymore? Is the portal even there?"

"Only one way to find out!" Cooper bolted toward the house.

"But . . ." Jess hesitated, but then, with a deep breath, she followed her brother's steps through the yard, up the rickety, warped wooden stairs, and through the unlocked back door.

The inside of the house was exactly as Cooper expected,

exactly the same as he'd seen it before. Jess, however, paused momentarily to stare at the debris, the broken furniture, the hole in the ceiling of the living room. All she'd seen for the last two months, after all, was the beautiful lie.

Cooper didn't slow as he crossed to the other side of the living room, skirting the old threadbare couch on his way to the front door. He put his hand on the cold knob and closed his eyes. If the other side of this door held nothing but Poplar Avenue, any and all chance of saving Elena and Gus was lost. He turned his wrist and opened the door.

Jess gasped.

The field of long yellow grass swayed in front of them, a gentle wind sending ripples through it like the surface of a pond. Cooper didn't waste a moment; he jumped over the threshold and onto the soft ground of the meadow. The sky was a piercing blue, and a hundred yards away stood the gilded door, still closed. He turned back to his sister and held out a hand.

Jess clutched the doorframe and shook her head slightly. "Cooper, what are we doing? What if we can't get back out?"

"Trust me, Jess. We'll be quick. We just need to find them!"

Jess didn't move but called out, "Elena? Gus?" Her feet stayed firmly planted in the house. Only the caw of an unseen raven answered her cry. "Cooper, what if we're too late?"

"We're not too late." There was no way he could know, but there was also no way he was going to step back through that doorway and give up. He owed Gus. He owed Elena. "We're the only ones who can help them. We have to try!"

Jess took a deep breath, then jumped. She landed beside her brother and held his hand tightly.

They took off running, both shouting Elena's and Gus's names. The wind pushed against their chests, slowing their progress, and the prairie grass snapped under their footfalls. The smell of summer hay rose all around them. And this time, the house trailed them; even as they ran, it seemed to remain a few yards behind. The golden door did the same. It was as if they were running on a treadmill.

But there were no cliffs, no oaks, no tea tables. And no Elena or Gus.

"Cooper, how long have we been running?" Jess eventually asked.

He had no idea. Seconds, minutes, years?

Jess spun around to scan behind them, only to stop running. She gasped, "Cooper!"

He pulled up, hopeful she had found Gus and Elena somewhere on the horizon, but instead saw Jess staring, horrified, at the house. He followed her gaze. The house was changing. The downspouts on the corners of the roof were melting away like hot wax, as if someone had lit an invisible wick at the top of each. At the same time, the roof began to sag in the middle, and the shingles were blurring together, smearing into one thick muddy slab.

"We need to go back!" Jess cried. "If the house is gone, we'll never get home!"

"No!" He shook off the thought. "We have to find them, Jess. We can save them!"

He began running backward, away from the house, and his heel caught on something large and soft. He toppled over backward, landing hard, flat on his back, the wind knocked out of him.

Lying on the ground beside him, almost completely hidden in the long grass, was the body of a girl, contorted in an unnatural position. Cooper looked behind him to see a second girl. "I found them. They're here!"

The two girls were nearly identical. They wore heavy woolen coats and leather shoes, and their hair was pulled back in braids. They looked exactly like the person Gus had become for that flickering instant on the bridge.

Jess came up beside him. "Oh my g—" she uttered. "Cooper, are they dead?"

"Please, no. No, no, no." This couldn't be how it ended. Not when they were so close. He scrambled forward to the side of the girl he had tripped over, placed a hand on her shoulder, and shook it gently. "Elena? Gus?"

The girl coughed in pain but didn't open her eyes.

"Jess! She's alive." He spoke gently to the girl. "Are you okay?"

Jess went to the side of the other girl. "Elena?"

"Cooper?" the girl next to Cooper moaned.

In an instant, the sky darkened to a shade of sickly green. A sudden clap of thunder shook the air all around them, leaving Cooper's ears ringing.

"Yes, yes!" Cooper answered. "It's me."

A bizarre echoing noise like a reverberating strum of the lowest string on a cello came from the house. Both Jess and Cooper turned to see that the chimney was now bent in half, seeming more like it was made of soft taffy than brick. The gutters were dripping as if clogged with rain, but instead of water, it was the metal itself plopping in huge molten drops to the ground.

"Can you . . . lay me straight?" the girl near Cooper said. She was trying to move, but it was clearly excruciating.

"Okay, okay," he said frantically. "Jess, move her arms and legs." Another painfully loud sound came from above them, but it would be hard to call it thunder this time. It sounded more like a head-on collision of two massive vehicles, echoing over and over.

Cooper and Jess each tended to one of the sisters as quickly as they could, all the while stealing glimpses of the disintegrating house. Their only exit.

When both girls were more comfortably situated, the first one finally opened her eyes. "What are you doing here?" she said, gripping at his shirt. "Cooper, you have to go home!" She turned and saw Jess. "Oh no!"

"It's okay. I think I know how to get you out of here."

The other girl was now able to painfully prop herself up on her elbows. She peered at the house and cried, "Dude! Are you nuts? Get out of here! Go!"

Cooper couldn't help it. He smiled. *Gus.*

"We'll go," Cooper said. "I promise. But first, tell me your names."

"You know our names," Gus said.

"No. Your *real* names! The names you were born with; the names of those two girls who went down on the ship all those years ago. The ones who were never mourned, who were forgotten."

The sisters looked at each other, then closed their eyes, like they were both trying to recall a dream long put out of mind. The girl who had been Elena put her hand over Cooper's.

"I'm Elizabeth. And that's Gwen."

A sudden blast of light and wind knocked Cooper and Jess over where they knelt, throwing them against the girls and bringing with it a smell of roses so strong, it made

Cooper dizzy. He had to shield his eyes from a blazingly bright beam that came from beside them, like someone was aiming a spotlight directly at their heads.

It was coming from the direction of the golden door.

Another ominous and unearthly moan came from the house. Its entire left side was now gone, melted down and seeping into the earth like a Popsicle left out in the sun. A violent wind began to swirl around them, battering the four of them from all sides.

The In-Between was enraged.

Cooper scooped an arm under Elizabeth's shoulders. She cried out in pain, but Cooper knew he couldn't stop. "Jess, help Gus! I mean Gwen!" Neither of them could carry one of the girls on their own, but after a moment Elizabeth and Gwen slung their battered and bruised arms over Jess's and Cooper's shoulders and stood. They all shuffled forward slowly, painfully, urgently. As they approached the stunningly bright light, Cooper had to close his eyes and lean into the gale-force winds that were trying to push them away.

When they were within feet of the door, Cooper heard the faint sounds of laughter beyond it.

"Gwen!" Elizabeth yelled. She reached a hand out ahead of herself. "It's open! It's truly open! I hear them!"

Cooper nudged her forward, hoping Elizabeth's own

legs would be able to support her for the final steps across the threshold. But she didn't move.

"Don't be afraid!" Cooper said. "Just go!"

But Cooper had misunderstood her hesitation. She hugged him tightly and spoke shaky words in his ear.

"Thank you."

Then she pushed away and took a wobbly step forward. She was gone.

Jess and Gwen came up behind him, and Cooper stepped aside. His clothes were beating against his body, whipped and twisted by the winds.

"Goodbye, Gwen!" he shouted into the howl, hoping the girl with braids beside him could still hear him.

"It's Gus, you goofball!" came the reply. It was unmistakably the voice of his friend.

The light was too bright for Cooper to steal a final look, but the two embraced and held on as long as they dared. Then Gus stepped back, and both Cooper and Gus said, "Thank you," at the same time. Though the hurricane winds threatened to steal their words away, Cooper held them tightly in his mind and heart. Then, once again, the two spoke together:

"Now GO."

Cooper felt Gus step through the door.

Then, in an instant, all went silent and dark. The wind ceased completely.

Cooper slowly opened his eyes. The door was gone. And while the storm had ceased, the scene around them was more terrifying than ever. The black sky was drooping down toward them like the top blanket of a pillow fort, threatening to collapse at any moment. He could barely make out the grass, if it could still be called that. Each blade was melting into an ever-growing straw-shaded puddle that stuck to his shoes. The distorted cry of a raven split the air, like it was coming from a toy bird whose batteries were dying.

The only source of light was the little window in the front door of the house. The right side of the building was dissolving before their eyes. It tenuously anchored the only part of the home that seemed undamaged: the door. Then, as more of the last remaining wall melted away, the door and its frame began to lean ominously, no longer secured by anything.

Cooper and Jess exchanged a terrified look before both streaking toward their only route home. When they were only a few feet away, the door and its frame started to fall toward them.

Jess cried out and shot ahead of Cooper, crouching as she approached. She let out a grunt as the door crashed against her back, coming to rest at a forty-five-degree angle across her. Cooper did a baseball slide to arrive next to his sister, yellow grass goo spraying out around him as he skimmed the surface like a Slip 'N Slide. Cooper reached up for the knob; then, huddled beside Jess, eyes closed, he turned it. With a click of the latch, the doorframe released and landed on the earth around them, passing over their crouched bodies.

The only noise in the eerie silence was their ragged breathing.

Then came a voice. "Hey! You two! What do you think you're doing over there?"

Cooper cracked open one eye. Beneath him, he saw gray, mealy slats of wood. He lifted his head and saw that he and Jess were lying on the back porch of the abandoned brown house. Mr. Evans was standing in the alley at the edge of the property with his hands on his hips, Panther at his side peering inquisitively at them, his black head tilted sharply to one side. Though Cooper could have sworn he still felt the doorknob, his outstretched hand was empty.

"Cooper, I know your mom has told you both to stay away from that house," Mr. Evans went on. "Get out of there. It's not safe."

You have no idea, Cooper thought. But what he yelled back was "You're right! You're totally right. It won't happen again."

Jess was now sitting up beside Cooper. She took in their surroundings before breaking into a huge smile.

Mr. Evans waited until they had stood up and begun moving toward the alley. Even once he started walking away, he glanced back a few times to make sure they were doing as they had said. Panther didn't budge from where he sat, and Cooper could have sworn the cat winked at him.

Once Mr. Evans was finally out of sight, Jess whispered, "We did it!" She wrapped Cooper in a hug.

He leaned in and hugged his sister back. "We did." The words from Gus's letter echoed in Cooper's mind: *You are both unforgettable. Never doubt that.* He had meant them for Cooper and Jess, but Cooper now knew the truth.

Those words were the key to saving them all.

32

Cooper and Jess found their mom, red and sweaty, stretching on a yoga mat in the living room, earbuds in, nodding happily to music they couldn't hear. She turned when she heard them come in, but her expression dimmed when she saw that Cooper and Jess were cut and bruised, their clothes ripped.

She rose and rushed toward them. "Oh my g— What happened to you two?"

Had it really only been a couple of hours ago that their mother had pedaled away on her bike? That Cooper and Jess had walked to the bridge? Their mom was clearly oblivious of all that had happened in that time.

"Mom, you should probably turn on the news."

For the next few hours, the three of them sat frozen on the couch as coverage from the bridge collapse dominated every news channel. Helicopter footage from every angle documented people escaping from damaged cars and precariously positioned vans and trucks. Cooper's mom wept as her children told her that they hadn't been mere bystanders to this awful event; they were survivors.

And she didn't even know about the In-Between. There was no way for Cooper or Jess to tell her that they'd never truly been in jeopardy on the bridge. They had, in fact, been marked for safety for months. The real danger had come when they'd risked getting stuck forever in an alternate dimension.

But that was more than Mom needed to know.

Over the next few days, every newspaper and website was filled with photos of the accident, interviews with survivors, and stories of the lives that had been lost.

It took three days for the most captivating news to emerge: the mystery of the two unidentified victims. A boy and a girl, wearing matching school uniforms that no one could identify. Day after day, the search for information continued, and Cooper wondered how it was possible that adults couldn't discover what he and Jess had. It had been hard to find, but not impossible, after all. But slowly the truth dawned on Cooper: the world was as blind to information about Elena and Gus as it had been to Elena and Gus themselves.

Soon interest waned. The headlines slowly gravitated back to disgraced politicians, sports scores, and celebrity news. Even two mysterious deaths couldn't hold the attention of a city for long.

They were sitting at breakfast a week later when their mother said, "I want to ask you guys about something. A reporter from the *New York Times* called me yesterday, wanting to interview you two."

"What?" Jess said.

"I don't know how she found out you were on the bridge, and I was about to tell her that you were not interested in speaking with her, but I wanted to at least ask you both before I did."

The New York Times. Their pictures and story would be seen all over the United States. The world, even. *We'll be famous the world over!* Jess had said what seemed like years ago now.

Cooper gave his sister an inquiring lift of the eyebrow. Neither of them needed to speak to know they agreed.

"Nah," Cooper said with a shake of the head. "We're good."

Their mother turned to Jess.

Jess smiled knowingly at Cooper. "Yeah. Everyone who needs to know our story already knows it."

During his downtime, Cooper went in search of delicious words for his journal. The front of it was now festooned with steadfast, camaraderie, fellowship. He drew pictures of himself and Jess that were vibrant and glowing. Visible.

Their mother's phone calls to the city were finally answered, and one day Cooper and Jess sat on the back stoop watching as a gigantic excavator demolished the brown house bit by bit, its rubble carted away one dumpster at a time. Every scrap of wood, shard of glass, and piece of foundation slowly vanished, ultimately leaving a bare, muddy lot. Only the swingless tree and one spindly little rosebush in the corner remained.

It was over. The mission was complete, all signs of the past had been wiped clean, and Elena and Gus—Cooper still had trouble thinking of them as Elizabeth and Gwen—were at rest. But Cooper nevertheless felt a small tug of unfinished business. Something he couldn't name was stuck in the back of his mind, like he and Jess were missing the closing act of the play.

"Their mom would have liked that," Cooper said a day later. He was standing at the kitchen sink, looking across the alley where Elena used to sit and stare at him.

"Liked what?" Jess asked from the kitchen table, where she sat doing homework.

"That rosebush," he answered. The plant was overgrown and thorny, brown from below-freezing temperatures, but still standing, despite the bulldozers. "Their mom had a garden."

Wait. Was *that* what they were missing? He crossed quickly to the junk drawer and began riffling through stray Post-it notes, paper clips, and takeout menus.

"What are you doing?" Jess asked.

"I think there's one more thing we should do."

"What are you looking for?"

Cooper didn't answer but motioned for her to follow him upstairs, where he turned in to Jess's room. He started opening her dresser drawers but still couldn't find what he was after.

"If you tell me what you need," Jess said, "I can help you find it."

"Aha!" Cooper walked to Mr. Miggins in the corner and tugged on the ends of the huge pink bow tied around the bear's neck, undoing it.

"Whoa! What are you doing?"

"Maybe we could just cut a piece of it instead," he muttered, not even hearing his sister.

"Cooper! What are you talking about? You aren't cutting any piece of Mr. Miggins."

"Well, of course I'm not going to cut *Mr. Miggins*. Just part of his bow."

Jess grabbed the ribbon out of his hand. "You aren't cutting anything until you tell me why."

"We need ribbon." Cooper couldn't remember exactly what he'd told Jess about Elizabeth and Gwen's last day alive. Elizabeth's final act before leaving home hadn't seemed that important a detail until now. "Just trust me."

Jess took a deep breath before slowly retrieving a pair of scissors from her desk. She hesitated for a moment, but when Cooper nodded reassuringly, she handed them over. "Just a little bit, though."

"Absolutely." Cooper lifted a portion of the ribbon and snipped. He carefully adjusted the remaining band of pink, recentered it around Mr. Miggins's neck, and tied a new, smaller bow. He proudly showed his handiwork to Jess. "How's that?"

She gave a thumbs-up in approval. "Now, tell me why."

As they walked downstairs, Cooper recounted the story, this time with every possible detail: the storm, the ribbon, the rosebush. "Elena, I mean Elizabeth, said, 'We bowed our heads for the only funeral our parents would ever have by those who loved them.'"

Jess smiled, nodded, and handed Cooper a pen from the kitchen counter as he flattened the piece of ribbon on its surface. In the best penmanship he could muster, he wrote:

For Elizabeth and Gwen

He handed the pen to Jess, and she added below Cooper's words:

You are remembered.

A sudden crash of thunder shook the windows. Jess's eyes went wide. "Where did that come from?"

Cooper looked at the closest window, where rivers of water were now running down the glass. "I guess a storm is needed for this sort of ceremony."

"But it's freezing out." Jess shook her head before gaping back at her brother. "That should be snow."

Cooper shrugged impishly. "I guess not. Let's go."

They went to the back door, and when Cooper opened it, a sheet of rain blew through the entry, soaking their clothes.

"This is crazy!" Jess yelled into the wind as they stepped out and closed the door.

Before they even reached the alley, they were both

drenched to the skin, though Cooper somehow didn't feel cold at all. There was no longer a picket fence around Elena's yard—there never had been—but they still entered the property where the gate had once appeared. Mud from the bulldozed earth oozed around their feet, clinging to their shoes in bigger and bigger clumps with each step.

They crossed to the rosebush in the corner of the lot. Blinking against the wind and rain, Cooper handed the ribbon to Jess and inspected the branches to find the worthiest bough. Finally he offered one to his sister. "Here."

Jess tied the ribbon in a sturdy knot, pulling the edges tight. Then she held her hand out to Cooper, which he gladly took. They stood there, hand in hand, faces turned up into the storm. In the flash of one final lightinng strike, the yellow house with blue shutters appeared, and the smell of pumpkin pie wafted through the air. Then it was all gone.

As quickly as it had come, the rain slowed, then stopped, and the calm that had eluded Cooper since they had left the In-Between finally settled.

"*Now* it's over." He put an arm around Jess's shoulders, and she put one around his waist. They watched the final rays of daylight disappear beneath the horizon. When darkness won out, Cooper said, "Jess, I think you need to talk to Mom about her date."

She slowly nodded and said, "And I think you need to

talk to Zack about coming over to hang out."

"You are absolutely right."

Jess grinned and rested her head on his shoulder. They slowly turned and walked, still hitched together, back to their driveway, past the garage and the garbage cans. Jess suddenly stopped and pulled away. "Hey! What is this doing out here?"

Beside the trash can sat Jess's mesh Giant Butterfly Garden. Cooper had heard their mother mumble that morning that it was finally time to get rid of that dud cocoon, and he'd assumed Jess had heard too. Apparently not.

Cooper walked toward the can and with a wink said, "Why don't we hide her in my closet? She probably just needs more time." As he reached for the green fabric handle, something else caught his eye. Glinting up at him from beneath the trash can, next to one of the big plastic rolling wheels, was something gold. He reached for it, and cold metal chilled his fingertips.

Cooper felt a little lightheaded as he stood, the butterfly garden in one hand, the plunger of his father's pocket watch in the other. The tiny ridges on its edges—like longitudinal lines on a globe—left a pattern in his skin as he squeezed it hard. The touch of that nub against his thumb was still comforting, even without the watch body it used to connect to. It was tarnished and bent and hardly distinguishable for what it used to be. Irreparable.

But Cooper still loved it. He put it in his pocket.

He held the butterfly garden out to Jess, but she gently shook her head and said, "I think Mom's right. Time to let it go."

Cooper waited to make sure she meant it before putting it back by the trash can. "Let's go inside. I'm cold." That was when he realized his clothes weren't wet at all.

They walked toward their house, and both faltered as their back door flickered. For a fraction of an instant, for one sparkling moment, it looked like something stolen from a king's castle or a czar's palace, intricately engraved wood embellished with ovals, twists, and whorls covered in gold leaf.

The two of them smiled widely. It was their turn to move beyond.

"Ready?" Cooper said.

"Yeah," Jess said with a squeeze. "I think I am."

"Five, four, three . . . ?"

"Two, one," Jess joined in. They didn't yell *Ouch!* The hurt necessary for this venture was already behind them. Together, they climbed the steps, opened the door, and stepped through.

As the door approached the jamb, it flickered one last time before gently clicking shut behind them.

Author's Note

When I was looking for inspiration for the magical mystery you just finished reading, I searched online for real mysteries, hoping that some event would serve as a starting point for my imagination. That's where I found the true, unsolved case of the Charfield railway disaster.

In 1928 an overnight passenger train headed for Charfield passed through a heavy mist, failed to heed a stop signal, and collided with a mail train at the Charfield station. Sixteen people died—but only fourteen of these people were ever identified. A girl and a boy, found together, were never claimed. No parent, school, or loved one ever came forward to name them or collect them. A headstone that includes

"Two Unknown" still stands in Charfield, England, to this day.

I read this with sadness and wonder. How on earth could two children leave this life in such a public manner without one soul knowing who they were? It was with this question that my story began.

In the course of writing and revising, I changed the Charfield mystery to involve only one anonymous child, and though one article I found about the disaster spoke of a school cap and blazer found in the train wreckage, the crest and the *Vigilantes Unum* banner are from my imagination. Just like the Charfield accident, the Triangle Shirtwaist Fire and the Sampoong Mall collapse are also real historical events. I have added names of fictional characters for the purpose of this story, but the other details of those catastrophes are true—there are many resources online and at your local or school library if you'd like to read more about them.

Turn the page to read
the first chapter of
REBECCA K.S. ANSARI'S

﹏ 1 ﹌

Charlie O'Reilly was an only child. It therefore made everyone uncomfortable when he talked about his little brother.

Liam. The kid who sang incessantly, left his dirty socks on the floor, and messed up Charlie's carefully arranged comic books. The one who both drove him insane and made him laugh until his sides hurt. *That* little brother.

But Liam didn't do that stuff anymore, because he didn't exist. And according to nearly everyone in Charlie's life, he never did.

"Please, Charlie," his father would say, removing his reading glasses and tipping his head to the ceiling. "Not again."

After a year of seeing that look on his father's face, Charlie learned to keep quiet. At home, anyway. But he had to talk during his visits to Dr. Barton's office, session after session, perched on her couch, the cushions dented by him and countless other troubled kids.

Dr. Barton had spent months explaining—in that tone that made Charlie feel like he was four years old instead of almost twelve—that his "imaginary brother" was a perfectly normal psychological response to "all the stress at home."

All the stress. The code words every adult used for Charlie's mother.

"People don't just vanish from everyone's memory, Charlie," Dr. Barton had said at their first session. "And your parents could *never* forget one of their own children."

But Liam had. And his parents did.

Charlie understood one important thing from his weekly sessions: no one was listening.

Today, however, was different. There was nothing Dr. Barton or his dad could say that would ruin Charlie's good mood. The next twenty-four hours held too much promise and hope for Charlie to let the doubters get him down.

"It's nice to see you in good spirits," Dr. Barton said over her cup of tea. She was tucked into her overstuffed leather chair, a perpetual electric waterfall burbling beside her. The sound of the waterfall was supposed to be soothing, but all it ever did for Charlie was make him need to go to the bathroom.

"Well, it's a big day tomorrow," Charlie said with a smile.

"I know—it's your birthday," she said.

"Yup. And one year to the day since Liam disappeared."

Charlie's father, sitting awkwardly beside him on the sofa, wilted at these words. Dr. Barton drew in a slow, deep breath.

Charlie knew what these sessions were about: to coax him into finally uttering, "Liam isn't real." Those three little words held the power to stop all the appointments, frustration, and hand-wringing. And as such, these sessions were pointless. Charlie would sit on this couch until he was eighty before he would say those words. Charlie's loyalty was stronger than whatever force had taken his brother away and wiped him from everyone's minds.

Just think of what we could accomplish if we spent this time acutally looking for Liam instead of sitting here blabbing, Charlie thought.

"As you know, Charlie," Dr. Barton said, "your father and I believe *something* happened last May. We just don't understand what, exactly. Why don't you tell us about that day one more time?"

3

Charlie stared at the bowl of fidget balls on the table between them. They had dissected his eleventh birthday countless times in Dr. Barton's quest to figure out what had "really happened." The truth, apparently, wasn't good enough.

He sighed. "When I went to bed the night before my birthday, Liam was there, in the bunk above mine. When I woke up the next morning, he was gone." Charlie recounted every detail: how the top bunk had vanished; how Liam's Legos and stuffed animals and posters and clothes and favorite cereals had disappeared from the house as cleanly as his existence had been scrubbed from everyone's minds. Charlie told the story slowly; they had an hour to kill, after all.

In each telling, Charlie offered up everything he could remember about that terrible morning and the days that followed. Charlie's dad would rub his back reassuringly as Dr. Barton ticked through her usual probing questions, most of them about his mom.

But she never asked about the night before, about what happened between him and Liam before they went to bed. Which was convenient, because Charlie was never going to tell her. That was none of her business. Only Ana, Charlie's best friend, got to know about that.

The fact that Liam's disappearance was Charlie's fault.

Finally Dr. Barton brought the session to a close with an

unsatisfied sigh. "Well, our time is up for today. I'll see you both next week."

Not if I can help it. Charlie popped up and headed down the hall, giving the adults the space they needed to whisper about him in the office doorway.

"Have a happy birthday tomorrow," Dr. Barton called after him.

"Oh, I will."

"Good work today," his dad said with a forced smile, the thud of the car door punctuating his last word. "I'm proud of you."

"Thanks," Charlie said, pretty sure the look on his dad's face five minutes ago hadn't been pride.

"Have you made all your birthday wishes, bud?"

I only have one, Charlie thought, but said, "Yup," instead. His dad thought all he wanted was a Nerf gun and a few comics.

They pulled onto the highway and Charlie watched the town of Kingsberg, New York, slide past in the purple early-evening light—new condos and shops mixed with old industrial buildings and warehouses, all under the ever-watchful eye of the old abandoned orphanage on the highest hill. *It's going to work,* he repeated to himself until they pulled into their driveway, past the crooked and sun-bleached invisible fence sign that no one had bothered to remove in the ten months since their Australian shepherd, Dipsy, had passed away.

"Can you get the door for me, Charl?" Dad said. "I still can't find my remote."

Charlie grabbed his backpack and hopped out. As he flipped up the plastic cover of the garage-door keypad, a fat, icy drop of water splattered on the tip of his nose. He looked up and almost caught the next drop in the eye. A blanket of blackened leaves clogged the gutter, dispensing yesterday's spring rain in little dive bombs. Green shoots stretched skyward from the eaves, having found a fertile home in the choked roofline. The weeds in the gutter mirrored those that were taking over the yard. Overgrown plants that Charlie's mother would never have allowed in her meticulously tended flower beds now thrived. The woody reeds of last year's lilies lay in a thick mat over the soil, and nothing but a few meager tulip shoots struggled toward daylight.

Charlie followed the car into the garage, stepped into the dark house, and immediately stumbled over something heavy in the mudroom. With a flick of the lights, his heart sank. Sitting by the door was his father's suitcase.

"It's just for a week, bud," his dad said, reading Charlie's face. "We're getting an exhibit on loan from the Smithsonian, and they need me in Washington, DC."

"You're not going to be here on my birthday?" Charlie said. He didn't care about parties or gifts, but he worried his father might need to be home for his plan to work.

His dad gently lifted Charlie's chin. "I hate it too, bud. I did everything I could to get out of this one, but there was no changing it. It's kind of a key part of the job."

Charlie looked at his dad and nodded.

"You know I'd be here if I could."

Charlie did know that. He knew a lot of things: that his dad's promotion at the museum of natural history meant a lot of trips out of town; that the raise that came with the new job was necessary to replace some of Mom's income; that he should be thankful they hadn't moved out of their house in Kingsberg to be closer to New York City. Knowing all of this, however, didn't make it easier. It seemed like his dad was gone more than he was home these days, and the geodes, T-shirts, and sharks' teeth that filled Charlie's room from museums around the world did nothing to make it feel less empty.

"As always, Ana and her folks are right across the street if you need anything," his father said, as if Charlie had forgotten where his best friend lived. "And I told Mrs. Gleason I'd be gone too, but I asked her not to check in on you this time without calling first."

Charlie grimaced. There was no catastrophe that could

inspire him to turn to their seventy-year-old neighbor. Even if she didn't smell like cigarette smoke and look like a bespectacled crested crane, she seemed just a little *too* interested in what happened in the O'Reillys' house. Apparently some people got pleasure from the misery of others.

"The exhibit should be pretty cool," his dad said. "It's a forty-eight-foot fossilized snake skeleton they found in Colombia. We'll go see it together when I get back."

"Dad. I hate snakes." Charlie pressed his lips together to stop himself from adding, "Liam loves snakes. You should take him."

"It's not like it's *alive*, bud. It'll be fun!"

Charlie wondered if his dad ever got tired of being so upbeat, the light that kept trying to penetrate the ever-present darkness in their house. It seemed exhausting.

"Anyway," his dad said, "I have the usual list of things to do while I'm gone. Why don't you go say hi to Mom while I grab some stuff from upstairs, and then we can go through it before I take off?"

Charlie nodded and walked into the family room.

Josie O'Reilly sat in her cave on the couch, staring at the television that hadn't been turned on in days. Her morning coffee was still on the end table, half full and capped in a skin of cold cream. Charlie clicked the lamp on and lowered himself beside her. He moved a clump of hair behind her ear and gave her a soft kiss on the cheek. Buried deeply under the musty odor of the unwashed hoodie she wore every day was the distant but comforting scent of Mom: Aveda shampoo, Dove soap, and something that always reminded Charlie of grapefruit. Even on her worst days—when everything seemed upside down—this fragment of the past calmed him. It gave him hope that his vibrant, adoring mother was right there, just under the surface, ready to spring back to life any day now.

A faint smile lifted the slack in her cheeks at his touch. "You're home?" she said. She was half under a blanket, her fingers tangled in the edge.

"Yup." He leaned in to her and wiped at his eyes. If it were years ago, she would ask him about his day, tell him she loved him, and throw her arms around him. Now, she sagged slightly under his weight. Charlie closed his eyes, knowing the ache in his chest would pass. It always did.

"Do you need anything?" he asked. "Want me to warm up your coffee?"

She shook her head.

After a few silent minutes, Charlie rose. "Love you." Her silence chased him out of the room.

Dad was a whirlwind of activity in the kitchen, packing up his carry-on and adding final notes to his list for Charlie.

He handed Charlie the scrap of paper, most of which was familiar at this point:

Drag the trash and recycling to the curb Monday morning
Do the dishes every night
Bring the mail in after you get home from school
Lock the doors and make sure all the lights are off before bed
Remind Mom to shower
Try to get Mom out for a few walks together

"What do these last two say?" Charlie asked, pointing at the bottom of the list. Despite inheriting his father's horrific handwriting, Charlie was no better at deciphering it than anyone else.

Dad looked over his shoulder. "Oh, the first one says pick up Mom's prescriptions on Tuesday. They can't fill them until then, but Lindsay and Donna at the pharmacy know you have permission to get them." He squeezed Charlie's shoulders and kissed him on the forehead. "And the last one says, 'Have fun on your birthday!'"

Charlie nodded and let himself be brought in for a hug.

"I'll see you next Sunday, okay? This should be the last trip for a little while, I promise." He waited for Charlie to nod. "Love you, bud. Take care of your mom."

And, with one last squeeze, he was off. Charlie watched

out the window as their ancient sedan backed out of the garage and his father tooted the horn in three short bursts as he drove away.

Dinner. Charlie's stomach growled as he crossed to the kitchen cupboard. He reached up to grab a box of spaghetti but found the shelf empty. He closed the cabinet and turned to the kitchen table, where he'd left the grocery list he'd made that morning.

"Mom!" Charlie hollered. "I thought you were going to get groceries today?" He tried to keep his tone light.

"Oh, Charlie, I'm sorry. I didn't get to it."

He knew Ana's mom could pick up groceries for them—she'd done it before—but he was tired of asking her when he could just do it himself; the store was a bikeable distance away. He wrote "groceries" at the bottom of his list of duties. He thought about adding birthday cake to the list on the table, but he couldn't bring himself to do it.

"I didn't get the laundry folded, either." Now his mother's voice rose in pitch, threatening tears.

"That's okay, Mom," he said brightly. "I'll do laundry after I eat, okay?"

Charlie was glad to hear nothing else from the family room. Silence at least meant no crying. Mom had been dealing with depression since before Liam left, but since he'd disappeared, it had gotten even worse.

Maybe she'll start to get better tomorrow, he thought. *When Liam's back.*

Charlie turned to the largely empty cabinet. Cereal again.

The clink of his spoon and the crunch in his ears was the soundtrack of dinner as Charlie leaned against the kitchen counter, bowl in hand. He turned the cereal box around so the Trix bunny would stop smiling at him, and a few minutes later he was putting his dish in the sink and heading down to the basement. He ignored the unwrapped Nerf gun in a Target bag on the floor of the laundry room, put his earbuds in, and got to work folding.

He emerged twenty minutes later, grunting from the weight of an overloaded laundry basket, to find all the lights out on the first floor. Mom had gone to bed. Charlie climbed the stairs and set the basket down quietly by his parents' bedroom door.

It was time.

He took down the New York Yankees poster from his bedroom wall, clearing the space Liam's Mets poster had once occupied. He then cleaned his clothes out of Liam's half of the dresser drawers. On top of the dresser, next to a stack of comics waiting to be sorted into Charlie's meticulously organized collection, was a photo encircled by a Yellowstone National Park picture frame. Three happy people beamed at him: Mom, Dad, and his own round eight-year-old self.

Liam's gap-toothed grin had once been in the photo too, but a bison's butt now occupied that space. Charlie had made Liam laugh so hard on that trip, he had shot juice out his nose and all over the back seat of the rental car. His parents had failed to see the humor.

Charlie grinned. He was totally going to make Liam snarf tomorrow.

When he happened upon the pair of pajama pants he had worn the night Liam vanished, Charlie stared at them for a moment. *It can't hurt, right?* He hurried to put them on, only to find they were at least three inches too short. His heart sank at the sight of his bony ankles. He wasn't the same person as he had been a year ago. He was taller, older. Sadder. *Not everything has to be exactly the same,* he tried to reassure himself.

As he brushed his teeth, he stared at the shelf where Liam's dumb baby shampoo used to sit. Somehow, despite being nine years old, Liam still hadn't figured out how to keep soap out of his eyes. Charlie scooted his own half-empty shampoo bottle over to make room. He glanced at the hallway mirror on his way to bed, his eyes catching on the spot where Liam had cracked it years ago during a tantrum involving a launched Matchbox car.

The glass was perfectly smooth. Like everything Liam related, it was as if he'd never existed.

Charlie's phone buzzed in his back pocket. A text from Ana glowed up at him.

What if it doesn't work.

He typed back: **It's going to work.**

If all it took was a wish, every one of my brothers would have vanished *long* ago.

Charlie smirked. **But did you ever wish it for your *birthday*?** ☺

It took a while for Ana's next text to arrive.

I get it -- if you could wish him away last year, maybe you can wish him back this year. But what if that dumb wish had nothing to do with it? Maybe it's not your fault.

Nice try, Charlie texted.

He knew what she was doing. Even though Ana, like everyone else, didn't remember Liam, she was the only one who believed Charlie. As such, she was also the only one who understood his disappointment and frustration every time he pulled a wishbone, tossed a penny into a fountain, or saw the first star of the evening. Each time a wish failed, it crushed him.

But none of those wishes was a birthday wish. The one that had made Liam disappear.